"This has got nothing to do with wisdom."

Liam released her only to bury his hands in her hair. "I've been wanting to do this all night. It ought to be made illegal for you to hide your hair. It's so soft."

Something swelled in her chest at the sound of awe in his deep voice.

Her hair slid through his fingers as he released it. His hands settled on her jaw, bracketing her face. The gesture struck her as tender…cherishing even. His head lowered over her and he spoke a fraction of an inch next to her lips.

"Tell me that you feel it, too."

Natalie couldn't squeeze a word out of her throat, so she just nodded once.

And then he was kissing her, and everything faded away.

Nothing existed but Liam's hungry mouth and her own erupting need.

Dear Reader,

It's the ultimate challenge to find meaning in the face of random tragedy. Truly, it's a hero's journey. Liam's and Natalie's love story is about traversing that difficult path, and in doing so, finding the faith to heal and love. I hope you enjoy this special couple's story.

You can find out more about the Home to Harbor Town series at www.bethkery.com, where you can also sign up for my newsletter and Yahoo reader group, or contact me via email, Twitter or Facebook. I'd love to hear from you!

Beth Kery

LIAM'S PERFECT WOMAN

BETH KERY

SPECIAL EDITION

Recycling programs
for this product may
not exist in your area.

ISBN-13: 978-0-373-65618-9

LIAM'S PERFECT WOMAN

Books by Beth Kery

Harlequin Special Edition

The Hometown Hero Returns #2112
*Liam's Perfect Woman #2136

*Home to Harbor Town

BETH KERY

holds a doctorate degree in the behavioral sciences and enjoys incorporating what she's learned about human nature into her stories. To date, she has published more than a dozen novels and short stories and writes in multiple genres, always with the overarching theme of passionate, emotional romance. To find out about upcoming books in the Harbor Town series, visit Beth at her website at www.BethKery.com or join her for a chat at her reader group, www.groups.yahoo.com/group/BethKery.

My heartfelt thanks go out to my agent, Laura Bradford, and my editor, Susan Litman. Thanks to both of you for believing in these story ideas. Sandy, Lea and Mary— thank you for the beta reads. I don't know what I'd do without you. Finally, love and thanks to my husband for your daily inspiration, patience and support.

Prologue

The beauty of a beach bathed in the glow of a midnight moon went a long way toward soothing Liam Kavanaugh's doubts about returning to his hometown after all these years. True, Harbor Town was hardly Chicago, and yes, the only danger he might face as chief of police of this lazy territory was falling asleep on the job during a monotonous workday.

But Chicago had nothing to compare to this view.

He walked on, his bare feet sinking into the cool, soft sand, letting himself be calmed by the sound of the waves breaking on the shoreline. Harbor Town had been the location of his childhood summer vacations. It would be where he would spend his next vacation, as well—a monthlong stretch of ease and relaxation before he started his new job.

Followed by a lifetime of ease? I'll probably become so relaxed I'll be practically comatose.

He stepped into the shadow of a tall sand dune, scowling at his thought. So what if serving as Harbor County's police chief was opposite on the crime-fighting spectrum from being an organized crime detective in the big city? He'd had his fill of life in the fast lane.

Hadn't he?

Every time he pictured himself as the local top cop it was as if he imagined a cutout, a facade, a caricature. Liam just wasn't sure he could "do" an Andy Griffith, small-town-sheriff type with any degree of believability.

He *would* do it, though. He had promised his mother and his older brother, Marc, that he'd quit the Chicago police department when he finished his latest undercover assignment, and he'd held true to his word. Marc always said the Kavanaughs had a tendency to try to undo their father's sin through hard work and community service, and Liam didn't necessarily disagree. Yet doubts about his new life lingered.

He cleared the shadow of a tall sand dune and came to a complete halt.

For a few surreal seconds, he wondered if he still lay in his bed in the cottage, sleeping. He shifted his feet, feeling his toes burrow through the soft sand.

No, he was awake.

But the woman before him was something from a dream.

She twirled and spun on the beach, an angel forged from moonlight. She seemed transported by her dance, at the mercy of the movement…compelled by some invisible force. Her body was supple, graceful and perfectly proportioned. Liam could easily make out the outline of it, scantily dressed as she was on the hot summer night. As his eyes adjusted to the dim glow of the moon, he made out a pair of shorts and a bikini top, but otherwise her limbs and torso were bare. Her hair was straight and longer than he saw most women wear it anymore. The ends of the tresses swished against her naked waist.

Her skin flickered in shadow and silver light as she moved

in her dance of solitary magic. She arched her back, her long hair touching the tops of her buttocks, her arms gliding through the air, her breasts thrust forward, as though she was seducing the moon itself.

A tingling sensation buzzed beneath his skin. He couldn't pull his eyes off the vision of ethereal beauty. Her arms stilled and she held the pose for a moment, while his breath burned in his lungs. Then her curving back straightened and Liam realized her dance was complete.

Suddenly, she was a mortal woman standing on the beach. An incredibly beautiful one.

Walking toward her, he called out. Her long, dark hair flew about her shoulders when she spun in alarm. Her face was cast in shadow, but Liam didn't need to see her expression to realize he'd frightened her with his presence. Harbor Town might be one of the safest places on earth, but no woman wanted to be accosted unexpectedly by a strange male past midnight in such a desolate location.

"No. Wait…I'm sorry. I didn't mean to scare you," he called out when she turned and ran inland, as quick as a startled deer. He resisted an urge to go after her.

There was no logical reason to pursue her when it would just frighten her more.

Still, as he watched the shadows claim her, he found himself longing to know her name.

Chapter One

Natalie Reyes placed her hand on her chest and applied a slight pressure, and old habit she'd acquired long ago to still her jangling nerves. She looked at the gold-and-glass clock on her desk.

Four minutes. He'd be here in *four minutes*. Or maybe he wasn't the type to be prompt, as confident and insouciant as he always seemed.

She must be stark-raving mad for calling him and asking him into the privacy of her offices…for planning on making him such a scandalous proposal.

Her anxiety mounted, and she froze when she heard a door open and close in the lobby. It was late for a workday. The two attorneys she shared office space with were already home, having dinner with their families.

So much for trying to forecast Liam Kavanaugh's actions. He'd come early.

Natalie sat up, ramrod straight. She'd tilted her small lamp toward the chair in front of her desk. Otherwise, the office was thick in shadow, thanks to the heavy drapes on the windows. It intimidated her to think of meeting him in the intimacy of darkness, but she'd be damned if she would display herself. Not to him.

The words were two of the hardest she'd ever uttered.

"Come in."

Her first thought was that he'd cut his hair since she'd seen him two nights ago. The tousled, blond mess used to be his hallmark. Natalie was stunned to see he looked impossibly more handsome with a shorter, mussed style. It looked darker now, almost brown in the dim light of the room. The goatee he wore was so short it was nothing more than a shadow that highlighted the cut of his jaw and his firm mouth.

She'd been wrong about his hair. His true hallmark was his eyes, which currently were spotlighting her with a cool, narrowed gaze. Gone was the carefree, charismatic playboy she remembered—in his place was a controlled, observant, slightly suspicious cop.

All the better. She wanted a professional for this job, after all.

"Please, sit down. Thank you again for agreeing to see me." She was pleased to hear that her voice didn't tremble.

"I still can't imagine why you wanted to," he said before he shut the door. Natalie jumped slightly at the brisk bang. She held herself unnaturally still as he sauntered toward a chair in front of her desk, all careless ease, a male animal in his prime who was supremely comfortable in his own skin. As he started to sit he leaned forward several inches, peering into the light cast by the single dim lamp on her desk.

Natalie moved subtly back into the cloaking shadows.

"I'm not accustomed to meeting strangers in dark rooms, Ms. Reyes. How do I know you're not planning to jump me?"

For a few seconds, she was too knocked off balance to

reply. His eyebrows went up in wry amusement and he leaned back in the chair. He, too, became shrouded in shadows with the exception of an angle of light that fell across his lower face, allowing her to see his mouth. It was a compelling mouth…decisive. Made for giving orders and laughing and…

Other things.

His lips tilted ever so slightly, as if he'd read her mind.

Cocky bastard.

"I can assure you I have no plans to 'jump' you, Mr. Kavanaugh," she replied with what she hoped was cold austerity.

"Too bad. A little action might have spiced up my evening."

"I'm sorry to have disappointed you."

He gave a slight shrug, ignoring her sarcasm. "No need to apologize. I'll get used to the slug's pace of Harbor Town before long."

"Do you already miss it, then?"

She sensed his muscles tensing despite his seemingly negligent posture. "What? My old job?"

"Yes."

"What do you know about my old job?"

She set down the pen she'd been nervously twisting in her lap. She could feel his gaze on her hand, which shone clearly in the pool of light cast by the shaded lamp.

"I'm friends with your sister-in-law, Mari. She's the one who told me you'd retired from your position at the Chicago P.D. and were returning to Harbor Town to become our police chief. Congratulations on your new position. We're very lucky to have a detective who has been decorated so many times and has so much experience." He remained unmoving and silent. She found herself leaning forward slightly into the light, trying to assess his expression.

"You don't believe me? Why?" she asked quietly when

she saw his lips were tilted slightly in skepticism...or was it derision?

"I'm sorry, I'm just finding it hard to believe you invited me into your office to welcome me to Harbor Town and extol my virtues. I'm a Kavanaugh, after all. You're a Reyes."

For a few taut seconds she heard nothing but her heart pounding in her ears.

"I'm an individual, Mr. Kavanaugh. Not a history."

He laughed, the low, rough quality of it taking her by surprise.

"Stop with the 'Mr. Kavanaugh.' I'm Liam."

"Fine. I'm Natalie," she replied breathlessly.

"And nothing against your individuality or anything, but I doubt even if you'd been marooned on a desert island for the past sixteen years you'd be unaffected by our history, as you put it. So why don't you just tell me why you asked me here tonight?"

Liam experienced a moment of regret at his bluntness when he noticed Natalie's hand go still on the blotter. She had beautiful hands. In the absence of any other visual information, he'd been focusing on them to a ridiculous degree. Something about their movement struck a chord of recognition in him. The woman he spoke to had a slender neck and dark, lustrous hair that stood in contrast to the pale suit jacket she wore. It gave off a subtle gleam when she shifted her head ever so slightly. The line of her jaw was firm, but delicate. Her shoulders were narrow and...*finely made*. He didn't know why the phrase popped into his head, but it seemed to fit. Her breasts were unexpectedly full beneath the soft blouse and tailored jacket she wore.

Slowly, he dragged his gaze away from that beguiling display of soft femininity. He was more than a little curious.

She was obviously a beautiful woman. So what was with the dark glasses, dim room and cloak-and-dagger routine?

It'd shocked him to the core when she'd identified herself on the phone yesterday. Up until then, one thing had been certain in his life: a Reyes didn't pick up the phone and call a Kavanaugh for a friendly chat.

He'd only been fifteen years old when his life had changed forever. It had been like a lightning bolt striking out of a clear blue sky. Sixteen years ago, his father, Derry Kavanaugh, had gotten drunk out of his mind one hot summer night and caused a three-way crash, killing Kassim and Shada Itani—his new sister-in-law's parents—along with Miriam Reyes, Natalie's mother.

Liam knew from his older brother's terse comments and his mother's tight-lipped fury that the lawsuit, and hearings following the crash had been especially bitter and ugly.

This whole situation with Natalie made him uncomfortable…edgy. He'd rather sit across a desk from a hit man with a rap sheet that stretched all the way down Main Street than this smooth-voiced female whose life had been altered by his father's crime.

"I'm very aware of the years of tension between my family and yours. There's no need to be flippant. Perhaps you're under the impression this is easy for me, Mr. Kavanaugh. If so, you're mistaken."

His eyebrows shot upward. A shard of steel had entered the cool silk of her voice. "So we're back to Mr. Kavanaugh, huh?" He sighed and shifted in the undoubtedly expensive, but uncomfortable, straight-backed leather chair. He cast his gaze around the luxurious office, trying to discern any details that would help him to better comprehend this strange meeting and cool woman. "Look, do you suppose you could just get to the point? Why'd you call me?"

Seemingly of their own volition, his eyes flickered down again over her breasts when she inhaled.

"I'd like to hire you," she said.

He raised an eyebrow. "Hire me? For what? I love my sister-in-law like crazy, but if Mari gave you the impression I'm up for spying on cheating boyfriends or roughing up someone who owes you money, she's dead wrong. Besides, I'm on vacation."

"I don't want to hire you to *rough up* anyone." He couldn't fully make out her expression, but from the sound of her voice, she was frowning. "You're a detective, aren't you? I'd like to hire you to do some investigative work. It shouldn't take much more than a few hours every day—probably less—and I understand you won't start your new job until next month."

"Oh, you've got it all figured out, do you?" he asked with a mixture of amusement and disbelief. "Do you mind if I ask just what it is you think I'm going to investigate?"

"The crash."

A silence settled between them like hot, flowing lead. It seemed to burn her cheeks, but her gaze didn't waver. She did start when Liam leaned forward suddenly, his elbows on his jeans-covered knees.

"*The* crash?" he clarified bluntly.

She nodded.

"Is this some kind of a joke?"

"No. I assure you I'm very serious. If you don't take the job, I'll hire another investigator."

A bark of laughter erupted from his throat. "Maybe you were too young to realize it at the time, but the state police conducted a full investigation of the crash."

"I know that."

"Do you?" he asked sarcastically. "Then what is it that

you expect me to investigate? What do you imagine I'll find, exactly?"

"I want to know why he did it."

He gaped at her. "Why *who* did *what?*"

"Your father. I want to know what was going through his head that night. I need to know."

He'd been insulted by plenty of men in his day, but not in such a personal way, and never by a woman who probably weighed a hundred and twenty pounds soaking wet. The fact that her voice never wavered, never trembled once, infuriated him.

"Do you really believe my father got in that car with the intention of causing a crash and killing all those people?"

She leaned forward, apparently affected by his low, dangerous tone. *"No—"*

"What, do you think he had some deep, dark suicidal and homicidal wish? You'd be better off hiring some crackpot psychiatrist if those are the type of crap answers you're looking for."

"I'm sorry. I didn't mean to insult you."

"You're doing a pretty great job of it, nonetheless," he muttered through a clenched jaw. He stood, ignoring the fact that she started in alarm at his abrupt movement. "Look, I know what my father did to you and your family. My dad made the hugest, most horrible mistake of a lifetime. He paid for it with his life, and my family has paid for it every day since then. I know yours has, too. That doesn't give you the right to ask me here and make nasty insinuations about his motivations. He was drunk. He caused an accident. End of story."

"Are you sure about that?"

He started. She either was the ballsiest woman he'd ever run into, the craziest or the meanest. Quite possibly she was all three.

"Yeah. I'm *sure* about that." Turning, he walked out the

door without looking back. But he had the impression that she remained behind her desk, frozen in the shadows.

Brigit Kavanaugh invited Liam and his sister Colleen to dinner at the house on Sycamore Avenue the next evening. After he'd filled up on his mom's fried chicken, Liam retired to the front porch.

He brooded as he listened to the familiar sounds of the neighborhood evening tree frog orchestra and the waves hitting the beach at the end of the street. When his sister joined him on the front porch, he couldn't help but notice she looked as irritated as he felt.

"Where're the kids?" Liam asked, referring to Colleen's two children, Brendan and Jenny. Colleen was a widow. Her husband, Darin, had been killed in service in Afghanistan three years ago.

"They're watching that new video Mom got them. So what're you frowning about?" Colleen asked grumpily before she plopped down on the porch swing.

"I was just thinking about the fried chicken. Do you think Mom is actually following her diet?"

Colleen's grimace told him she'd been wondering the same thing. Their mother had had a mild heart attack last year. At Brigit's latest checkup her doctor had told Colleen her mother had been neglecting her medications and ignoring her dietary restrictions. The news had stunned the Kavanaugh children, who had thought their mother was perfectly healthy.

"I *think* she is." Colleen gave the screen door a furtive look. "I check with Margie at the pharmacy, and she says Mom has been picking up her medicine regularly. She only had one piece of chicken tonight, and she used vegetable oil to fry it."

Liam sighed. They couldn't follow their mom around like she was a two-year-old and make sure she followed doctor's orders, after all. Brigit Kavanaugh was a warm, caring mother. She was also a well-guarded fortress when it came to her private life.

"I told you why I was frowning, so you spill about why you're in such a bad mood," Liam challenged his sister. "Oh, wait…I've got it. It's Wednesday evening."

Colleen pulled a face as she twisted her blond hair and clipped it at the back of her head. She didn't respond, but she didn't have to, really. His comment explained everything. Eric Reyes, Natalie's older brother, volunteered at the facility where Colleen worked as a clinical social worker. Being around Eric tended to make Colleen a tad tetchy.

It wasn't that Liam or Colleen didn't understand Eric's and Natalie's anguish over the loss of their mother. It wasn't even that they begrudged them for their suit against their father's estate or the court order that resulted, whereby the majority of Derry Kavanaugh's savings and property had to be liquidated to pay the Reyes and Itani families for damages. It was Eric Reyes' insolent attitude whenever he encountered a Kavanaugh that really got to Colleen—and Liam, for that matter.

Unfortunately, Reyes volunteered at the Family Center— the treatment facility and organization for victims and survivors of substance abuse that Mari Kavanaugh had opened last year. Liam had learned from experience that his sister would likely be in a bad mood on Wednesday evenings, since Eric worked at the center on Wednesday afternoons.

"What'd the prince of physicians do this time to get your knickers in a twist?" Liam asked.

"He trumped me with one of my clients."

Liam whistled under his breath. Colleen and Liam were close. They were only fifteen months apart in age, and they'd gone through a lot together as the two youngest Kavanaugh children. He could easily tell his sister was on a low boil at the moment, and he knew why. Colleen fought like a lioness for her clients. If he cared two cents about Eric Reyes, he'd actually feel sorry for the idiot for stepping into her clinical territory.

"I can put up with his cocky attitude. I *have* put up with it. But if he thinks he can mess with my clients or my course of treatment, he's got another think coming," Colleen said.

"Seems as if the Reyes family is stepping up the feud a tad."

Colleen glanced at him sharply. "What do you mean?"

"I had a strange request for a meeting yesterday."

"From who?"

"Natalie Reyes."

Colleen's aquamarine eyes went wide. "What in the world did she want?"

Liam glanced warily at the screen door, worried his mother might overhear. When he heard the distant clatter of a dish in the kitchen, he spoke in a low voice, giving Colleen the major details of his meeting with Natalie. She stared at him, obviously as stunned as he'd been.

"I don't understand," Colleen said when he'd finished his explanation. "What does she hope to accomplish by having someone investigate the crash—*you,* of all people? It happened sixteen years ago."

"You're telling me?" Liam asked wryly. "I was blown away when she said it."

"What was Natalie like?" Colleen asked curiously, after a moment. "She's so quiet. I've lived in Harbor Town for most of my adult life, but I've only caught glimpses of her in the distance. She works in that office downtown, but she's practically a recluse."

"She might be the solitary type," Liam muttered, "but she's every bit as annoying as her brother. She's a block of ice."

"And…"

"What?" Liam asked. He was confused by his sister's manner—intense but hesitant at once.

"How bad was the scarring?"

Liam just stared at her. When Colleen took in his expression, she clarified. "On her face. It was in all the papers and news following the crash. Don't you remember? The left side of her face was..." Colleen sighed sadly and began to rock back and forth on the swing. "They had photos of her in the papers. She was a beautiful little girl before the crash. That's what a fair portion of Dad's estate went toward. The judge ordered it for Natalie's reconstructive surgery and compensation...if the surgery didn't work."

Liam blinked. Suddenly Natalie's tendency to hide in the shadows made perfect sense. He didn't want to believe it, for some reason, didn't want to even consider what his sister had just said.

His mother had sequestered Liam and Colleen—her two youngest children—in Chicago after the crash, where the media clamor had been muted. He recalled few details from that gray, grief-filled time. They'd stayed in Chicago until Brigit had lost their family home in the lawsuit, and they'd relocated permanently to the vacation home in Harbor Town. By that time, the sensationalized reports in the news had tapered off, even if the memories and sometimes harsh judgments of the townspeople hadn't.

"Liam?" Colleen prompted when he didn't speak.

"I never saw any scars," Liam replied hoarsely.

Colleen shook her head so that a portion of her long, thick hair fell from the twist on her head and coiled down her shoulder. "I'm not really sure what Natalie's intentions were, but I do know it's not uncommon for a trauma survivor to feel a need to make sense of what happened to them. Natalie Reyes was the only one who lived through that accident, after all," Colleen said.

She sighed and kicked on the floor of the porch, sending the swing into squeaky motion. "If she struck you as cold, I'd imagine she comes by her aloofness honestly."

The muscles in Natalie's left eye began to twitch under the constant strain. She placed her hand over the scarred portion of the eyelid and pressed gently, trying to alleviate the familiar discomfort. Shutting the folder on the monthly financial reports for the Silver Dunes Country Club, she glanced at the clock. It was going on nine. She wasn't tired, but her damn eye was, and that meant her work day was over whether she liked it or not.

A sigh of relief leaked between her lips when she flipped her desk lamp to the dimmest setting.

She started at the sudden sound of a knock on the door, her hand falling to the desk. When the loud rapping resumed after a pause, she stood.

Who in the world was knocking? It was about the time Erma often began her night cleaning, but Erma had her own keys. Perhaps she'd forgotten them?

She hurried through the dark, silent waiting room, seeing a tall figure through the frosted glass of the front door. The outline was definitely not that of her short, stout cleaning lady. She hesitated before she flipped the lock.

"Who is it?"

"Liam Kavanaugh."

Her hand moved clumsily as she fumbled with the lock. Why had he come back? Over the past forty-eight hours, she'd come to terms with the fact that she'd handled their meeting the other night all wrong. Natalie was only used to dealing with people in the cut-and-dried language of business and numbers. She didn't have much of a social life. Of course she had a few friends, like Mari Kavanaugh, and she and her brother, Eric, were very close.

But she wasn't "good" with people. And she had little experience in dealing with a man like Liam Kavanaugh.

Strike that. She had *no* experience in dealing with a man like Liam.

"Hello," she said breathlessly after she'd swung open the door. A distant streetlight allowed her to see him. He stood on the sidewalk wearing a dark blue T-shirt and pair of faded, worn jeans that looked as if they'd been tailor-made for his body. All the Kavanaugh children had been natural athletes, Natalie recalled. Something about Liam's balanced stance and long, lean frame reminded her of that.

Twilight made it difficult for her to read his expression, but she saw the gleam of his eyes beneath his lowered brow.

"Can we talk for a minute?" he asked.

She nodded. Even if he'd come here to castigate her more for her request, he was here. She'd have the opportunity to explain herself better. Despite her desire to do just that, nervousness bound her throat as she led him to her office. She immediately darted behind the safe fortress of her desk but looked up in surprise when Liam blocked her by standing in her path. He stood closer than she'd expected.

She flinched and began to step away, but he stopped her by encircling her wrist in his hand. He'd lowered his head. Her upturned face was less than a foot away from his. She stared at his cotton-covered chest, not really seeing anything. Instead, panic started to rise in her as she inhaled his clean, male scent.

"You never really answered me the other day—about what you hoped to discover with an investigation of a crash that happened sixteen years ago," he said quietly.

"*You* never really gave me the chance."

She shut her eyes briefly in regret. She could tell by the increased tension in his gripping hand that he'd been offended by her quick, sharp response.

"I'm sorry. I didn't mean to sound so defensive," she murmured, her voice barely above a whisper. She went back to studying his chest, trying to gather herself. "Maybe...maybe it's difficult for you to understand my reasons."

"Try me."

Why did he persist in holding her? His touch unnerved her, as did his nearness, and this confession was difficult enough as things stood.

"I think a lot about what was going through your father's mind on that night of the crash. You might think that my... obsession about it would have eased over the years, but it hasn't. It weighs on me." She lowered her head, blocking herself even more from Liam's laserlike stare. "Maybe you'll think it's foolish, but it's like an unhealed wound. It bothers me, not knowing what motivated him on that night. What made a father of four children, a successful lawyer and businessman, get behind the wheel of his car with the equivalent of twenty drinks in him? I wasn't trying to insinuate he purposely caused the crash the other night," she assured in a pressured fashion. "But there *had* to be some reason he was in the state he was. If I knew...if I could at least understand, maybe I could finally let it go."

"Knowing wouldn't change anything, Natalie."

She blinked. His tone had sounded warm...concerned, even? She forced herself to remain still, her head bowed, even though she longed to look up at him in that moment and try to discern if his expression matched his voice.

"Maybe you're right. But I need to try. I've talked it over with Mari. She said she's read that it's not uncommon for survivors of trauma to need to know all the details that led up to the event. It's necessary for the grieving process...to make sense of things."

"My sister Colleen said something similar. Does that mean you're still grieving?"

This time she did look up—slowly. Standing as close as they were, she could make out his features despite the shadows. His expression was currently completely sober, as if his features had been carved from rock. The veins in her wrist seemed to swell and throb beneath his fingers.

"I'm done grieving. But it's as if a few crucial pieces are missing from my life. I can't seem to stop thinking about filling in those gaps."

"Why *me*, then?" he asked after a moment.

"Mari has spoken so highly of you," she whispered through leaden lips.

"And?" he prodded.

"I thought…I thought perhaps you might share some of my desire. To know the truth," she added quickly.

His mouth quirked sardonically. "And of course it wouldn't hurt that as a Kavanaugh, I might have some inside information."

Her spine stiffened. What he'd said had pricked her. Her curiosity about Derry Kavanaugh was so great that it *had* appealed to her, this idea of having access to someone who knew so much about him.

"I'd considered it," she said honestly, "but not in the unflattering light you seem to be imagining. Think whatever you want. You will anyway."

For a few tense seconds they just stared at one another in the dim office. Natalie became hyperaware of the steady movement of his chest as he breathed in and out.

"Okay. I'll take the job."

"You will? That's…that's—"

It happened so quickly that she never had warning. The fluorescent overhead lights flared on, and her eyelids shut automatically at the unexpected intrusion. Still stunned, Natalie struggled to blink as a spasm went through the muscles of her left eyelid. It drooped involuntarily.

"Ms. Reyes," Erma called out in surprise. "I didn't realize you were in here!"

"Turn out the light," Liam barked.

Natalie caught a fleeting image of a shocked-looking Erma standing just inside the open door of her office. She glanced up. She clamped her eyes closed, but not before the image of Liam Kavanaugh's hungry stare was stamped permanently in her mind.

The light switch clicked, and the room was suddenly dim again.

"Are you all right, Ms. Reyes?" Erma asked, sounding anxious and contrite at once.

"Yes. Yes, of course. I'm fine," Natalie murmured, barely holding down a rising tide of emotion. "We'll be out of here in just a moment, Erma."

"No problem. Like I said, I'm sorry for interrupting. Are you sure you're okay?" She felt regretful for the anxiety in Erma's voice. Natalie's mother had been a cleaning lady and she was always extra considerate and respectful of Erma, knowing from experience how exhausting and solitary the work could be.

"I'm fine, Erma," she said, using all her effort to keep her voice even. She kept her face averted. "Really, I am."

Natalie heard the door shut. She jerked her arm, suddenly wild to get away from Liam, all of her usual tight control evaporating to mist. A sound of misery escaped her throat when instead of releasing her, he embraced her.

Chapter Two

"Calm down," he said near her ear. "It's okay."

The unexpected eruption of emotion that shuddered through her flesh mortified and bewildered her. Plenty of people had looked at her face before. Plastic surgeons and doctors had scrutinized it, photographed it and even written medical journal articles on it. Townspeople constantly cast curious, furtive glances her way at the grocery or drugstore.

Why was she crying just because Liam had seen her scars?

Maybe it was because none of those other people pinned her with such a piercing, honest gaze that made her feel so exposed.

"Just leave, please," she muttered as she tried to pry herself out of his arms.

"Okay. Okay, I'll go. But give me a second."

Natalie paused in her struggling. Her breath seemed to burn in her lungs at the sensation of his long, jeans-covered thighs pressing against her own. It was a new experience for her, to be held against such a virile man. Her thoughts seemed to flit around her head like panicked moths trying to escape from her skull.

He cradled her jaw. She went entirely still when he brushed the pad of his thumb along her cheek. The movement mesmerized her, and she stared fixedly at his chest, afraid to raise her gaze, but never so aware of another human being in her life.

"The bright light hurts your eye?" Liam stated more than asked.

"You don't have to feel sorry for me," she blurted out angrily.

"I wasn't feeling sorry for you," he said, sounding slightly insulted. "I asked you a simple question. If we're going to be working together, I want to know."

"The muscles are weak in my left eye," she murmured after a moment, contrite for her defensive reaction. "It tires easily. It's sensitive to bright light."

She sensed his nod of understanding. He resumed stroking her with his thumb.

"Is that why you prefer going to the beach in the moonlight?"

Her head jerked up, but she instantly regretted her move. His mouth was only inches from hers.

"What do you mean?"

"I saw you the other night. Dancing on the beach."

She just stared at him. How could he have recognized her? The beach had been draped in shadow. She'd known him, but surely that was different. She had long practice in recognizing Liam, especially on a beach, where he seemed to belong.

"How…when did you realize it was me?" she whispered.

"Just now," Liam said. She felt his warm breath mist her lips. "I knew you once I fully saw your beautiful face."

What sort of a game was he playing?

She backed out of his embrace, experiencing an over-whelming longing to get back on track…to return to a place of control. Something told her it was downright dangerous to allow Liam the upper hand in this business endeavor…to get the upper hand, period. He probably didn't think twice about saying she had a beautiful face or touching her as if it were as natural as breathing. Liam had always been a ladies' man. The idea of him treating her in the same way he did other women panicked her.

This time when she attempted to put her large, solid desk between them, he didn't stop her. She impatiently dried her tears with a tissue and pulled a checkbook from her desk drawer.

"What are you doing?" he asked, sounding bewildered and a little irritated.

"We haven't yet discussed salary," she said as she wrote rapidly. She ripped out the check and held it up for him to take. "This is your retainer. I'll pay you twice that amount when the investigation is complete."

It annoyed her that he didn't take it because her hand shook slightly, making the check tremble in the air. Erma had taken her off her guard by switching on that light, but Liam had shocked her to the core by embracing her. She'd thought she knew what she was doing by making this proposal, but apparently Liam wasn't something to be quantified and controlled.

"How will you know if I've investigated the matter fully or not?"

"I've heard about your work ethic from Mari. I've read about your career. You've been a champion for victims of crime…for discovering the truth. If there's anything relevant to be found, you'll do your best to uncover it once you take this check."

"Chances are I won't be able to uncover anything. I want you to know that up front."

"I understand. I still want to try," Natalie stated, her firm tone belying the fact that she couldn't meet his eyes.

Liam stared at the check uncertainly.

He'd run the gamut of emotion in the past few minutes, and now Natalie had the nerve to make him feel even more. He'd leaped at the opportunity to see her face, then experienced a rush of guilt for his curiosity…his hunger. It wasn't seeing her scars that made him feel guilty, it was her palpable vulnerability.

The bone structure of her face was as finely made as her body. Natalie's wasn't a run-of-the-mill beauty, but the haunting kind. There were several smaller scars near her temple, but the most prominent was a half-inch-thick one that ran all the way from her eyelid and disappeared below her hairline. It only seemed to highlight the perfection of everything else about her.

It saddened him, that scar—saddened him on a bone-deep level. It was a reminder of the months and probably years of pain that a young, innocent girl had endured.

But his sorrow didn't blind him to the beauty of the woman beneath that scar. In fact it only added to it.

His father had caused this; he'd been responsible for making this exquisite woman shrink into herself like she'd thought her face would actually harm an onlooker.

Seeing that had hurt him in a way he couldn't quite put into words.

For a few tension-filled seconds Liam considered telling her to keep her money. Natalie Reyes was far, far from being the devil, but somehow making this pact with her intimidated him.

Accepting that check sealed the deal.

For sixteen years, Liam had struggled to create a cohesive image of his father. He'd loved his dad like crazy. All four Kavanaugh children had. He'd been charismatic, fun... someone he'd always respected. It'd been a trial for Liam to come to terms with the drastically different pictures of his father that he'd received after the crash: the laughing, powerful patriarch...the selfish, heartless drunk...

Who the hell was *Derry Kavanaugh?*

Part of him had always been curious about what had happened that night. He shared that same internal pressure as Natalie Reyes. Problem was, he'd been disillusioned by his father once—when he was fifteen years old. Taking that check from Natalie would set him on a path where he might discover even uglier truths about his dad.

He hesitated on a knife's edge. Why did he waver now when he'd dived headfirst into drastically more risky and dangerous situations in the past?

The image of Natalie sitting behind her desk, cloaked in shadow, penetrated his awareness. For some stupid, incomprehensible reason, he wanted to walk behind that desk and undo the knot at the back of her head. He wanted to fill his hands with that glorious spill of hair he'd seen on the beach and here in her office the other night.

It irritated him, this dichotomy of feelings she inspired in him. He wanted to shake her sometimes. He also wanted to protect her. Most of all, he wanted to tear through her facade so he could lay bare that woman he'd glimpsed on the beach.

He must be losing his mind.

He reached out and swiped the check.

"I'll make a report to you when...*if* I get anything of substance. Which I doubt very seriously," he said pointedly before he walked out of the office.

A few days later Natalie was putting some groceries in her trunk when her cell phone rang. Her heart leaped with a mixture of anxiety and excitement when she noticed the identity of the caller.

Ridiculous. She really needed to get past this girlhood crush she'd had on Liam Kavanaugh. She wasn't that girl anymore. Children had a license to dream, and Natalie knew how dangerous dreaming could be for a grown woman.

"Hello?" she said as she got into her car. She'd planned to drop by her brother, Eric's, place and maybe make him some dinner with the groceries she'd just purchased.

"It's Liam. I was wondering if you want me to give you periodic reports on what I've found."

"Oh…I don't know. I hadn't really thought about it. Have you found something important?"

"No. Well…maybe." He made a sound of impatience. "Problem is, I don't know what you'd think is worthwhile or not. What are you doing right now?"

"I'm in the Shop and Save parking lot. I just finished some errands."

"Why don't you swing by my place? I stained the hardwood floors earlier, but we could talk out on the terrace." When she didn't immediately respond, he added, "I won't take more than twenty minutes of your time."

She felt contrite. She was the one who had proposed a business arrangement between them. Why would she hesitate to meet with him? A voice inside her head taunted her, accusing her of being gun-shy because of that embrace the other day, but Natalie willfully ignored it.

"Of course. What's your address?"

He gave it to her. Natalie had lived in Harbor Town her whole life, so she knew precisely which house he referred to.

"You bought the Myerson cottage?" she clarified.

"Yeah. I know what you're thinking."

"You do?" she asked in numb amazement.

"That I'm a sucker for buying a money pit like this? My

mother keeps telling me I'm nuts," he said, wry amusement
in his tone.

"No...no that's not what I was thinking at all."

She told him she'd be there shortly and hung up the phone.
Less than ten minutes later she pulled past an old mailbox—
even *that* was rich in character and craftsmanship—and drove
down the long, weedy gravel drive. It was late August, the
time when nature was at her ripest. The Victorian-era cottage blended almost seamlessly into the overgrown landscape,
thanks to the thick surrounding foliage and blooming vines
that covered the stone exterior. Flowers were everywhere—
bluebells, wisteria, daisies and roses.

It had stunned her to hear he'd bought the cottage, but understanding slowly started to mute her incredulity.

This place was as wild and untamed as Liam himself.

She heard the sound of the waves breaking in the distance
as she got out of the car. *Of course.* She hadn't been far from
here that night when they encountered each other on the lake-
front. The Myerson cottage was just south of White Sands,
the public beach where Liam had come upon her in a private
moment. Perhaps like her, he hadn't been able to sleep that
night.

She started toward the door but paused when Liam came
around the corner of the house, poking his arms into a short-
sleeved button-down shirt. She froze at the sight of him. He
was far enough away that she was granted several seconds to
study him through the lenses of her dark glasses. He wasn't
bulky muscular, but he was *ripped*. There wasn't an ounce of
fat on his torso, just lean muscle and smooth golden-brown
skin. He wore a pair of casual cargo shorts that fastened low
on his narrow hips. The omnipresent braid of leather encircled his wrist. The white shirt he threw on looked delicious
next to his tan. His legs were long and well-shaped and dusted
with light brown hair. From the light sheen of sweat on his

abdomen and chest she guessed he'd just come from doing some physical labor.

"Hi," he greeted as he approached, buttoning his shirt with fleet fingers.

"Hello," she replied, mentally damning her breathlessness. She slammed the car door and walked toward him, glad that he closed the shirt over his bare chest. He was almost indecently gorgeous. She noticed a small smile pull at his mouth when he came to a halt.

"What?" she asked warily.

"I'm not used to seeing you in your civilian clothes."

She glanced down at her attire—jean shorts, canvas tennis shoes and a blue-and-white-striped tank top.

"Strike that," he said. She lifted her head. Her breasts tingled beneath his flickering gaze. "You weren't in civilian clothes that night I saw you on the beach. You weren't wearing much of anything, were you?"

Heat rushed into her cheeks. It confused her to the core, this tendency he had to say things and make it sound so warm…so intimate. It shouldn't surprise her, of course. Liam Kavanaugh was a born flirt. He probably just didn't know how to shut it off, even with an unlikely candidate.

"I wasn't expecting anyone to see me on that night," she said, trying to sound matter-of-fact. It wouldn't do to let him believe their chance meeting on the beach had meant anything to her.

"Obviously."

She inhaled slowly. It certainly didn't take him long to make her feel like she was floundering.

"Accountants deserve downtime as much as police officers," she said stiffly.

"More so," he agreed with a shrug. "If I had to wear a suit every day to work I'd go nuts. I'd dive into my jeans the second I walked out of the office."

He looked surprised when she laughed, but she couldn't seem to help it. "Or your board shorts, no doubt."

His smile was like sex distilled. Her laughter faded at the sight of it.

"I think you might be getting the hang of me, Natalie."

"Heaven forbid."

He chuckled appreciatively as he waved for her to follow him on the ancient stone path that circled the cottage. "Is it all right if we sit out here?" he asked, waving to the shaded terrace at the back of the house. "The fumes from the stain are fading—I've got almost every window open in the house—but they might still bother you."

"Of course, it's lovely out here," Natalie replied, meaning it. She followed Liam up some stairs, appreciating the view of a sparkling, light blue Lake Michigan.

"Something to drink?" he asked. "I have iced tea, soda—"

"No, I'm fine. Please get something for yourself, though," she said as she sank down onto a cushioned deck chair.

"I'll be right back."

Natalie nodded and leaned back in the chair. It was hot today, but the humidity had dropped. The view was amazing from there on the stone terrace—the tall prairie grass and colorful flowers in the backyard swaying in the gentle breeze, the waves hitting the rocky beach. She envied Liam. It was two years ago that *she'd* almost bought the Myerson cottage. She'd fantasized once about taming these surroundings into a cottage garden. Well, not *taming*, really—who would want to cultivate such a wild, glorious place? Her brother had been very uneasy about the idea of Natalie living in such a secluded spot though, and Natalie hated the idea of him worrying about her. In the end, she'd bought her cozy town house instead.

It was the practical thing to do, but sitting there on the terrace, she couldn't help but feel a very illogical longing.

"If I didn't know I was in Michigan, I'd swear I was on

the English coast," she told Liam with a smile when he came through the screen door. She automatically took the iced tea he offered her, momentarily forgetting she'd said she didn't want anything to drink. "It looks so similar."

"Does it? I've never been," Liam said as he plopped down in the chair that faced hers. His blue eyes were fixed to her mouth. She suddenly felt foolish for saying something so whimsical and took a sip of her tea.

"So what it is it you wanted to talk to me about?"

"Right. To business," Liam said drolly.

"That is why you called me, isn't it?"

His small shrug seemed to say that the reason would have to do.

"I don't know how much you know about my father, but you knew that he was a lawyer," Liam began.

She nodded. "He was the legal counsel for Langford, a defense contractor and publicly traded company. He'd worked there for over twenty years."

"You've done your homework."

She lifted her chin to face him. It must seem odd to him to know she'd gathered as much information on his father as she could over the years.

"I've told you how curious I was."

He nodded slowly, his eyes steady on her face, before he took a swallow of tea and set down his glass on a wrought-iron table.

"Then you might know that for a half year before the accident, the Securities and Exchange Commission had been investigating Langford for fraudulent financial statements. As chief counsel for Langford, my father was a major part of that investigation."

Her pulse began to throb in her throat. She'd wondered about this very issue. Was Liam saying that his father had acted so irresponsibly on that night sixteen years ago because he knew he might be implicated in Langford's fraudulent practices?

"I had heard about it," she said quietly. "Just an occasional reference here and there in some old news clippings about the crash. The SEC came out several weeks after the accident and announced that no charges would be made following an investigation at Langford. I thought no wrongdoing was found."

"There wasn't any wrongdoing," Liam said soberly.

"Then...why are you telling me this?"

He paused to take a sip of his tea before he continued. Natalie found herself admiring the muscular movement of his tanned throat as he swallowed. She guiltily met his gaze when he spoke.

"I'm telling you because I figured that you, like most people, would have come up with some sort of conspiracy angle when they heard about the SEC's investigation. It goes something like this, I can imagine—Derry Kavanaugh swindles thousands of honest shareholders with fraudulent financial reports. When he gets caught by the SEC, though, he can't stand the prospect of his family and the public knowing he's nothing but a dirty criminal. He'd rather die than face the music. So he gets smashed one night and in the process of offing himself, selfishly takes three other lives as well."

Her cheeks burned at his seemingly casual recital. Maybe he'd stated it bluntly to make a point, but what he'd said was true. She *had* wondered if something akin to that was behind Derry Kavanaugh's erratic actions that night. Despite her embarrassment, she refused to be cowed by Liam's subtle sarcasm.

"I'll admit I wondered about the SEC's investigation. Even if he'd been innocent, your father might have been overwrought. The investigation had gone on for months. That's a terrific amount of pressure to live under, especially when he had to keep working and putting up a brave front. Many people would crack under stress like that."

She paused, feeling self-conscious when Liam said nothing but just studied her, his long legs bent before him and his arms sprawled on the sides of the chair. Beneath his seeming insouciance, she sensed a diamond-hard edge, however, a tension that belied all that relaxed male brawn.

It made her wary, this difficulty she had in reading him. Was he angry?

"How do you know that wasn't the case with your father?" she persisted, despite her uncertainty.

"Because my father knew that the SEC wasn't going to level any charges at the time of the accident."

"What?" Natalie asked, sitting forward. "But the SEC didn't announce that until weeks after the crash."

"True," Liam said briskly. "But I accessed Langford's financial disclosures. The details of the investigation are in the files. The SEC had finished their investigation and made their determination weeks before the accident. The announcement just wasn't made to the public until a stockholders' meeting several weeks later. As chief legal counsel, my father knew the SEC's decision as soon as it was made. I have a dated memo that proves that fact. My father definitely knew Langford was cleared of any wrongdoing at the time of the accident."

"I see."

"Disappointed?" he asked.

"No. No, of course not," she said, irritated. How could he be so warm at times, and at others, downright confrontational? "I want the truth, not easy answers."

Something about the tilt of his mouth before he took another swallow of his tea made her think he doubted her.

"Can I ask you a question?" she asked impulsively.

"Sure."

"Did you already know what you just told me, or was it news to you?"

He shooed a buzzing fly away with a lazy flip of his hand before he answered. "I knew, but in a family-knowledge kind of way. I wasn't sure of the facts."

"What do you mean?" Natalie asked. She leaned forward even farther in her chair. She couldn't help it. She was sitting with a man who had known firsthand the secrets of the Kavanaugh house. Things that Natalie had wondered about incessantly were common knowledge to Liam.

Something sparked in his eyes when he noticed her curiosity…her eagerness.

"So this is the part where it's handy to have an inside man for your investigator?" he asked softly.

"It's not bizarre that I would want to know what you know."

His nostrils flared slightly as he studied her, but then he sighed and glanced toward the lake. The sunlight reflecting off the water seemed to make his eyes even more electric blue than usual.

"True. But your interest makes me uncomfortable. People tend to keep family stuff close. Until Mari Itani came back to town a year ago, we hardly ever mentioned the crash amongst ourselves. Hell, my sister Deidre took off after the crash and hasn't been back to Harbor Town since, let alone sat around for chats about our father getting bombed one night and killing himself and three other people."

Guilt seeped into her awareness. She wasn't the only one who carried open wounds. For a few seconds, she wasn't sure what to say.

"You wonder if I've asked you to unlock Pandora's box," she said quietly after a moment.

His gaze narrowed on her, and Natalie realized she'd been

correct in what she'd said. This *was* the source of the conflict she sensed in him.

"My mother told us when we were young that people might make snide comments about Dad being mixed up in fraud soon after the accident. She was right. Kids can be cruel. They overhear their parents saying stuff, and they might not understand the content, but they get the tone. My mom prepared us by explaining that the investigation at Langford had showed no wrongdoing. Until you asked me to look into matters officially, I had no way of proving what my mother told us, though. Now I can. I've seen the records." He flashed a hard look before he took a sip of his tea. "Turns out that my mother was right all along. My father didn't have a meltdown on that night because he thought he was going to be exposed as a crook."

"Do you really think I'm disappointed because you didn't discover some dirt on your father?" she asked incredulously.

His teeth flashed white in his tanned face, but he hardly looked amused. "It would have been a convenient story for you. Something to hang your hat on."

"I told you I was interested in the truth, whatever that may be," she countered. "I'm not your enemy, Liam. I'd like to think we're on the same side."

"It might seem like we're on the same side until I uncover something that makes my father look worse than he already does. Did you ever think about that when you cooked up this little scheme?"

She sat rigid in her chair. His voice had been quiet, but she sensed his volatility.

"I didn't do this to take your memories of your father away from you. If it's true that you discover something about him that you don't like in this process, I'm sorry. More sorry than you know. But if that were the case, it wouldn't be me that changed the way you thought of your father. It would have been *him,* Liam. And you…because you were honest enough to look for the truth."

His stare burned all the way down to her heart, but she didn't back down.

"I hired you for several different reasons," she continued in a hushed tone, "but the main one was that you search for the truth at all costs. That's the conclusion I came to after I spoke with Mari and after I read all those articles about your undercover work that exposed all those corrupt cops."

He abruptly collapsed back in his chair, the palpable tension in his muscles dissipating. He exhaled heavily.

"I hope you made a good decision," he said.

"I did. Besides, has it ever occurred to you that the opposite might occur?"

His drawn brows told her he wasn't following.

"You might uncover something that makes you understand your father better than ever before. You might gain an even clearer picture of Derry Kavanaugh. Perhaps you'll be able to love your father more…not less."

Something flashed in his eyes that she couldn't interpret. For a few seconds, only the sounds of the waves hitting the beach and the birds twittering in the trees reached her ears.

"How long have you danced?" he asked abruptly, taking her by surprise.

"What?"

A lopsided grin tilted his mouth. "How long have you danced?" he repeated slowly. "It's pretty obvious you've been doing it a long time. You're very talented." His gaze turned warm. "I had no idea accountants could be so…flexible."

She blushed. Damn him. His was turning the focus of the conversation onto her to keep it off himself. He constantly made her feel like an awkward adolescent. And he did it without effort. She sipped her tea and glanced out at the lake, squinting behind her sunglasses.

"I told you no one was meant to see that. It's not very kind of you to keep bringing it up," she said coolly.

He looked genuinely confused by her statement. "I'm not being unkind, I'm just…fascinated."

She turned to him, her lips parted. "Fascinated? By what?"

"By you. Does that surprise you?"

"Yes," she said quickly.

He laughed after a second. She couldn't imagine why *he* seemed so bewildered when *she* was the one who was utterly baffled.

"So…how long? Have you danced?" he clarified when she just continued to gape at him.

"I started ballet when I was eight years old," she said.

"You're good enough to do it professionally. Don't you want to?" he asked matter-of-factly.

She was the one to laugh this time. "Forgive me for saying so, but I don't think you're much of an expert." When he quirked his eyebrows at her, she laughed some more. "I like to dance for fun. I still take lessons. It's a hobby, but I think it'd be a monumental mistake to quit my day job."

His shrug seemed to say he'd let her have her way because he didn't want to ruffle her feathers any more than he already had. Natalie decided that it was imperative to bring this conversation back to professional matters.

"Liam—" She paused when he tensed. His steady gaze unnerved her. "What…why are you looking at me like that?" she mumbled incredulously.

"It's nice…the way you say my name. So, where were you going when I called you?" he asked. Natalie blinked. Had he really just said he liked the sound of her saying his name with so much heat, and then switched the topic as casually as if he was making a comment about the weather?

"I was on my way to my brother's. I was going to make him dinner, if he was available."

"Why don't you let me make you dinner instead? I grill a mean steak and make a mediocre salad."

"That's not necessary—"

"I know it's not necessary. I want to. Why are you so surprised by that?"

"It'll take more than Liam Kavanaugh offering to cook a meal to surprise me," she shot back in the midst of her rising confusion.

Her breath caught when he leaned forward and examined her through a narrowed gaze.

"You're not being honest," he murmured, his light tone belying his X-raying gaze. "You're surprised that I want to have dinner with you. Why would you be surprised that a man would want to have dinner with a beautiful woman, Natalie?"

Chapter Three

He'd give anything to comprehend what was going on in that brain of hers. One second she was acting like a skittish colt and the next she was saying something deadpan in that low, sexy voice of hers, reminding him for all the world of a sophisticated Bacall baiting Bogie.

She was a puzzle, and the detective in him needed to figure her out.

Liam bit off a potent urge to ask her to take off her glasses. He knew she wore them to protect her sensitive eye, so he refrained. Barely. They'd sat there and talked for the past half hour and almost the entire time he'd been hungry to look into those soft, dark eyes… When he wasn't admiring her elegant arms, or the slope of her shoulders, or her legs or her firm, full breasts.

He felt guilty about it, but he wasn't really sorry that the cleaning lady had switched on that light the other night. He was greedy. If that light hadn't gone on, he wouldn't have been gifted with the vision of Natalie's exquisite face and huge, startled eyes.

He wouldn't have sacrificed that.

Why did he have this almost overwhelming need to touch her again, like he had the other night? She'd quivered in his arms like a shaking leaf, but she'd felt so soft.

She'd fit against him perfectly. He couldn't quiet the desire to explore every nuance of that fit.

It was a mistake to ask her to dinner. He saw how tense she'd gone at his suggestion and he sank back in his chair.

"It's just dinner, Natalie."

"I know that," she replied quickly.

He felt bad. Gone was the impenetrable woman with the quick tongue. She seemed flustered. He thought it would be prudent to give her some space to gather herself. He stood. "I'll go and defrost some steaks and then take a quick shower. Are you going to be okay out here for a few minutes?"

"I…yes, but—"

"Great, because I'll be back before you know it. I'll tell you the rest of what I found out over dinner."

"There's more?" she asked, sitting up straighter.

Bingo, Liam thought. He'd hit the right button. He wondered, though, when she spoke next.

"Don't defrost the steaks," she said suddenly. Liam was positive she was about to say it would be prudent for her to leave.

"I was just at the grocery store. I have steaks in the car. If we don't eat them, they'll go bad."

He forced himself not to grin too widely as he asked her for her keys and went to retrieve the meat.

While Liam showered, Natalie wandered through the yard and climbed out onto the rocky breakwater that partially surrounded the small beach. The breakwater seemed ancient.

Natalie wondered if it had been created by the cottage's first owners. She stood on a slick slab of dark gray granite, breathing deeply of the fresh air.

"Don't fall. Those rocks are sharp enough to do some damage," Liam yelled from the terrace.

Natalie spun around. He stood on the terrace, his hair still damp from the shower, the wind causing his blue cotton shirt to billow around his torso. She hopped from one rock to another and rose up the incline to the terrace.

"The wind has really picked up," she said as she sprang up the steps. She paused when she saw his expression. She smoothed several loose wisps of hair that had escaped her bun, suddenly self-conscious under his stare.

"Hmm," Liam mused as he regarded her. "Guess I don't have to warn you about falling on the rocks. Might as well tell a gazelle not to be clumsy."

Embarrassment and pleasure flooded her in equal measure. She glanced away. "Why don't you let me make the salad? I can do a few grades better than mediocre."

"Sure, if you don't think you'll mind the smell."

Actually, the odor from the floor stain was barely noticeable and Natalie said so when Liam led her into the house. Thanks to all the open windows and the wind coming off Lake Michigan the house smelled as fresh as a wild meadow.

"Oh!" she exclaimed in surprise when she followed Liam into the kitchen. "You didn't tell me you put in new cabinets. They look wonderful. And the floors…they're gorgeous," she said, peering into the empty dining room just off the kitchen.

"Thanks," Liam said. "How'd you know the cabinets were new?"

"Oh…I looked at the cottage several years ago when I was shopping around for a place."

He chuckled before he opened the new stainless steel refrigerator and started pulling out supplies for a salad. "You're a lot smarter than me if you didn't buy it."

"Oh, no. Don't say that. This house is amazing."

"What made you decide not to buy it?" Liam asked as he straightened and shut the refrigerator with a thump. He deposited an armload of vegetables near the sink.

She shrugged and wandered over to where she'd spotted a knife block with a wooden cutting board turned on its side against the back of the countertop. "Oh, you know…it's not a very practical place for a single woman and all. My brother didn't think it was a great idea."

"What did *you* think?" Natalie was highly aware of him watching her as he leaned against the counter. He now wore a different pair of cargo shorts and a loose blue T-shirt that brought out the color of his eyes and seemed to make his tan glow. He hadn't put on any shoes. He was the picture of sexy summertime ease. She made a point of avoiding the appealing image of him as she withdrew the cutting board.

"I think this place is brilliant," she said, smiling. "I used to sneak over here when I was little and wander around. No one lived here for over twenty years."

"Maybe prospective buyers didn't like the bats that were flying around in the attic," Liam said dryly.

She made a face. "The real estate agent never showed me the bats."

"That's a shocker."

She smiled and removed some juicy-looking tomatoes from a sack. "I never saw them as a kid, either. When I was nine years old, not even bats could have convinced me this place wasn't enchanted. I'd sneak away when my mother took us to the beach and dozed off. There's a path that runs from White Sands to here."

"I know."

She glanced up when she heard the huskiness of his voice.

"I took it the other night. That's when I saw you dancing," he said as their stares held.

She looked away. There it was again. He kept bringing up that moment he'd spied her dancing on the beach. It'd been a perfectly innocent occurrence. Natalie couldn't imagine why it felt as if Liam was reminding her that he'd seen her naked every time he brought it up.

"Strainer?" Natalie asked briskly.

He turned and opened a cabinet, removing both a stainless steel strainer and a white salad bowl.

"Natalie."

She glanced up as she reached for the items.

"I can close the shades if the room is too bright."

She blushed. "Don't bother. I'm fine. The tint of my glasses alters to the brightness of the light." She turned on the water and began rinsing the vegetables, highly aware the whole time of Liam looking down at her. He'd said she fascinated him earlier. Was he, perhaps, one of those men she'd encountered infrequently over the years who confused pity for attraction? Given their circumstances, Liam might feel an even stronger tendency for misplaced pity.

Natalie wasn't unrealistic. Men had been interested before. She wasn't the worst catch on the planet. It wasn't her facial scars that stood as a barrier to her having relationships with men. No, it was the way the scars had interfered with a normal social development that had done that. She'd been on the brink of adolescence during those excruciating months in the hospital. Girls at that age were highly concerned about their appearance. Compound that natural self-consciousness with a traumatic head injury, multiple broken bones and facial wounds that had made half her face look like ground beef before the surgeries—not to mention a mother, a lifeline, who had been ripped away from her during that critical period—

and the makings of a socially awkward adult woman were all in the mix.

"I'll go and throw the steaks on the grill," Liam said a few seconds later. Was it her overactive imagination, or did he seem disappointed in her sudden fascination with clean vegetables?

She mechanically went about her task. Most of her brain was busy telling her foolish heart to slow. She shouldn't have agreed to have dinner with him. This curiosity about his father and the Kavanaughs was tempting her to venture farther and farther into intimidating, unknown waters.

No, that wasn't honest. It was her fascination with Liam that was risky.

Natalie had never slept with a man. She knew she was a bizarre anomaly in this day and age—a twenty-seven-year-old virgin. Liam, on the other hand, was the most confident, gorgeous man she'd ever imagined, let alone encountered. The idea of Liam and her engaging in any kind of sexual mating dance was just...*ridiculous.*

"We're going to get rain," Liam said as he entered the kitchen ten minutes later, carrying two grilled steaks.

Natalie nodded as she set the knife down on the cutting board. In fact the natural light in the kitchen had grown dimmer and the wind had started to howl across the dunes and the rocks, causing the window blinds to rattle. "We should go and shut your western windows."

"Yeah, I guess we should," Liam said as he set down the steaks on the counter. "You get the downstairs ones and I'll get upstairs?"

They met back in the kitchen a few minutes later, the sound of the wind now a distant wail. Natalie was finishing setting the round oak table in a nook in the kitchen when he returned.

"Is this okay? I know you planned to eat outside, but—"

"No, this is great," Liam enthused. He hadn't seemed to notice the awkwardness that had settled on her when she realized how intimate the setting was—the approaching storm, the cozy kitchen, just the two of them sitting down to a meal. He was so comfortable in his skin he didn't know how to recognize self-consciousness in others, Natalie thought.

He placed the steaks on the table next to the salad and walked over to the refrigerator. "Is iced tea okay?"

"I already poured us two glasses. They're chilling off."

"Excellent," Liam murmured with a satisfied grin as he brought the glasses over to the table.

"It looks like it's possible you weren't bragging when you said you made a mean steak," she said as they sat down together. Liam took her plate and began to serve her. Rain began to spatter on the windows.

"I never brag. Only the absolute truth ever leaves these lips." He'd said it so soberly, but his sudden grin was pure devilry.

"We'll see."

His eyebrows quirked in interest at her challenge, and Natalie thought she understood why. With another man, her reply would have sounded cool. For some reason with Liam, it had seemed like she was flirting.

She rolled her eyes and picked up her knife and fork.

The beef melted on her tongue. He'd cooked it to perfection. He was gentleman enough not to say anything out loud, but the look he gave her read loud and clear—*I told you so.*

They both started to talk at once.

"Why did you let your brother talk you out of buying this place?" he asked.

"What else were you going to tell me about—"

She broke off when his question penetrated her awareness. She smiled a little uncomfortably and took a bite of salad.

"Personal before professional," Liam said before he stabbed his fork into the meat.

"I didn't let Eric talk me out of moving here. I came to the conclusion this place was too much work for me."

"Uh-huh," Liam said doubtfully.

Thunder rumbled outside.

She paused and sat back in her chair. "Why do you say it like that? Do I seem like that much of a pushover?"

He took a swallow of his tea. "Not at all. I've just heard about your brother. He has a reputation for having...strong opinions," Liam said with the air of someone who was choosing his words carefully.

"And this *reputation* you speak of," she said slowly. "Was it, perhaps, provided to you by your sister Colleen?"

He studied her for a moment before he forked some salad. "Let me guess. Eric has given you the opinion Colleen is a bit of a steamroller herself."

She laughed when she saw the sparkle in his eyes.

"Maybe they're both a little right," Natalie murmured, still grinning. "I wouldn't call Eric a steamroller, necessarily, but he's very decisive. And he worries about me a lot. Too much, really, but I understand. He was eighteen when we lost Mom and I was only eleven. We don't have any other family here in the states. My father died in Puerto Rico soon after my mother discovered she was pregnant with me. She and Eric came here with practically nothing but the clothes on their back and my mother's dreams of giving her kids a chance for something better than she'd ever had."

"What did your father die of?"

"Cancer. I never knew him," Natalie replied quietly. Wind-driven rain struck the panes in earnest now. She raised a bite of meat to her mouth and glanced at Liam. "Are you and Colleen close?"

"Yeah, we are," he said unabashedly.

"And what about your other sister, Deidre?"

Liam nodded. "The three of us are all close in age—eighteen months between Deidre and Colleen, fifteen between Colleen and me. But Deidre hasn't really lived in Harbor Town since she went to college. She was always working in other towns on her vacations. She was an army nurse for years, but recently she became a civilian. She's still got wanderlust, though. She's working in a hospital in Germany, at the moment. We talk as much as we can, but it's hard while she's overseas. Deidre is actually one of the reasons Marc and my mom pressured me to leave the Chicago P.D."

"What do you mean?"

Liam grinned crookedly. "Okay, I was exaggerating a little. But before Deidre was in Germany, she spent two years in Iraq and Afghanistan. It was hard enough for my mom worrying about whether or not I was getting shot on the streets. Knowing Deidre had bombs exploding around her hardly made for peaceful nights for her."

"It doesn't surprise me," Natalie said before she reached for her glass.

"What doesn't surprise you?"

"You becoming an organized crime detective…or Deidre ending up as a nurse serving in combat. You guys were always such daredevils. I remember how Deidre performed in that water show on Mackinac Island during the summers."

"Yeah. Deidre's an excellent trick skier. My dad taught her. He taught us all."

"He did?" Natalie asked, unable to contain her curiosity over this tidbit of information about a man who had remained such a puzzle to her.

Liam nodded. "He and his brothers were all naturals in the water—swimming, diving and skiing."

Natalie paused, digesting this novel information about Derry Kavanaugh. When Liam glanced at her, she thought she might have seemed too curious, so she kept the topic on a safer playing field.

"Every little girl in Harbor Town thought Deidre was a goddess. I did. She was so cool I couldn't even fathom her." Natalie smiled in reminiscence.

"Really? You knew who Deidre was?"

"Of course. Everyone knew the Kavanaughs in Harbor Town."

"Did you know me?"

"I knew who you were." The "safe" topic had quickly veered into dangerous territory. "Now…I answered your question from before. You answer mine."

"I'd rather hear what you thought of me."

"I'm sure you would."

She stilled when he leaned toward her and spoke in a mock-serious, confidential manner. "I'd really rather hear about the girl doing the thinking."

After a stunned moment, she laughed. She couldn't help it. No matter how much she knew she should keep a distance from him, Liam's charm was impossible to ignore. He chuckled right along with her. She suddenly became aware of how close he was to her. His teeth were even and straight. Some orthodontist had made a mint off of Liam. He had a deep dimple in his right cheek. She could see the thousands of points of color in eyes that reminded her of the sea on a sunny day—cerulean blue with green, aquamarine and topaz interspersed, adding to their depth and brilliance.

His smile faded. His brows drew together. He straightened and focused on eating his meal, suddenly looking serious and even a little fearsome in his intensity.

A thick silence settled. Natalie resumed eating as well, even though her taste buds didn't seem to be working any longer. Liam had undoubtedly remembered the purpose of their meeting wasn't fun and laughter. It wasn't as if they were old school friends or lovers. No, they were members of two families with a shared history of tragedy and strife who had joined together, albeit warily, for a very somber mission.

Natalie was glad Liam must have realized that as they sat together, eating dinner while rain spattered on the windows.

She'd do well to recall the same.

The rainstorm blew out as quickly as it had rolled in. By the time Liam had loaded the dishwasher and Natalie had straightened the counters, the sun was poking through the clouds, making the wet rocks on the beach and breakwater gleam.

The uncomfortable tension that had settled between them had never really faded while they finished their meal. Natalie found herself longing for escape. She was about to tell Liam she needed to stop by her office to see to a few important items when Liam shut the dishwasher and stood to his full height.

"Now that the rain stopped, let's go out on the terrace. I'll tell you the other thing that might—" he threw her a warning glance "—or might *not,* be important."

"Okay," Natalie said, her curiosity piqued, despite his attempt at downplaying things.

The lounge chairs were still beaded with raindrops so Liam and Natalie remained standing, both of them gazing out at the lake which was mostly gray except where shards of sunlight created bands of light blue. The quick storm had brought a drop in temperature. A breeze off the lake caused Natalie to shiver. She rubbed her hands up and down her bare arms to warm herself, all the while noticing that Liam seemed unaffected. He stared out at the lake, his arms crossed below his chest, his bold profile fixed and thoughtful.

"I guess you probably know that my dad was at the Silver Dunes Country Club bar before the accident."

"Yes," Natalie said softly, aware of the sensitivity of the topic. "The Club was investigated for overserving him."

"The club was cleared of that charge," Liam said. "My father had several drinks there, but witnesses and the bartender said he didn't appear drunk, just quiet. Sullen." He glanced swiftly over at her. "The Silver Dunes had a video camera mounted over the bar. The film was used to investigate whether or not the bartender or the Silver Dunes had any culpability in my dad's intoxication and allowing him to get behind the wheel of a car that night."

"Your father's insurance company's attorneys used the video in the hearings as well," Natalie added in a hushed tone.

Liam nodded, his expression rocklike. "Right. The insurance company tried to use the tape to say it wasn't possible that my dad was as intoxicated as the suit suggested, and therefore was not as reckless as was alleged. The bartender served him three drinks in the span of an hour and a half. Not ideal, but not enough to make a six-foot-four-inch, nearly two hundred pound man looped out of his mind. But the lab reports don't lie. If my father hadn't gotten tanked at the Silver Dunes Country Club that night, he'd poured enough booze down his throat later on to get a platoon ripped."

Natalie closed her eyes briefly when she heard his bitterness.

"Where's that video now? Does it still exist?" she asked breathlessly.

"It exists. I just found out for sure this morning. I have a couple of friends who work for the Michigan State Police. The videotape is still catalogued in evidence storage."

"Can we see it?" Natalie asked incredulously.

"*I* can."

She started slightly when she again recognized his volatility. It once again struck her—this time like a stinging slap—just what it was she was asking this man to do.

She swallowed the lump in her throat.

"If you decide you don't want to watch that tape, I'll completely understand."

"Would you?" he asked woodenly, still staring at the lake.

"Yes. I would."

His eyes were narrowed into slits when he turned toward her. "I said I'd take this case. This is a viable piece of evidence, and I wouldn't even consider overlooking it."

Natalie opened her mouth to protest, but something in his expression made her pull up short. She inhaled slowly and stared down at the damp stones of the terrace. This is what she'd hired him for, after all. It was ridiculous to feel regret that he was doing his job.

"All right. Please let me know if you find anything important," she said.

"I'll do that."

She gave him a shaky smile, not making eye contact, and waved toward the path at the side of the cottage. "I've stayed much longer than I planned. I really should be going. Thank you so much for dinner."

"You're welcome," he said.

Natalie closed her eyes briefly in defeat. She really had irreparably insulted him by asking him to take this job.

Why had he accepted it, then?

"Well, I'll see you," she said awkwardly.

"Have a good night."

Liam's deep, rumbling voice seemed to vibrate in her mind as she hurried around the corner of the house. She felt such a bewildering mixture of emotion that her chest ached with it. Was she really surprised he'd turned distant? She was the one who had hired him to relive old, painful memories. Surely she couldn't expect him to adore her for that.

Still, it hurt, his abrupt coldness there at the end. Her heart leaped, making her catch her breath when she heard Liam call out to her.

"Yes?" she asked, turning around.

She stood next to her car, the tension in her building by the second as she watched Liam walk toward her. It was a little like watching that storm rush the beach a while ago. His face was impassive but his eyes looked every bit as wild as a summer tempest.

He reached for her.

"Liam?" she asked, bewilderment and wonder mixing in equal measure in her query. He leaned down over her so close that she inhaled the intoxicating scent of clean male skin and spicy aftershave. How could his lips look so hard and determined and yet so sensual at once?

"Just one more thing before you go," he said, his voice husky.

He leaned down and seized her mouth in a kiss. Natalie swayed on her feet, knocked off guard by the heat and power of Liam Kavanaugh striking her in a flood of sensation.

After a few seconds, desire burned away Natalie's shock. He caught her against his body.

And she was swept away by the storm.

Chapter Four

He'd approached her like a conqueror, his mouth firm and very persuasive. But as soon as he felt her melt against him, he gentled, as if he were apologetic for the onslaught on her senses. He used his lips like a blind man uses his fingertips to know his world, discovering the shape and texture of her mouth through his sense of touch. He sipped, he nibbled; he sucked at his leisure. His mouth slanted unevenly over hers, sandwiching and caressing first her upper and then lower lip. She shivered uncontrollably when he bit with exquisite care and dragged his white teeth over the sensitive skin of her lower lip.

He took advantage when her lips parted with a sigh and entered her neatly, his tongue searching, seeking, stroking. She found herself responding in kind, stroking him back tentatively at first...then not so tentatively.

The kiss turned hot and wild, like a spark igniting in a forest of dry timber.

Liam shifted his hips, pressing her bottom against the trunk of her car. A wave of heat flooded her body, making her dizzy. He continued to kiss her as if his existence depended on it. Maybe it was that imperative, because if he stopped, Natalie wondered if she'd be able to draw breath from the unpleasant shock.

His hands swept down her body, skimming her ribs and the sides of her breasts before they encircled her waist and finally settled on her hips. He hooked his fingers into the belt loops of her jean shorts and tugged. Their bodies slid against each other as he gave a low, vibrating groan, and Natalie thought she knew why. He'd just cradled his hardness against her softness. It'd been like he'd shifted them into a perfect template…a divine fit.

Natalie touched his shoulders as their tongues dueled. Excitement surged through her when she felt how tense he became in response to her caress, how he pulled her gently, but also almost desperately against the hard angles of his body.

She felt strange—as if she'd been plunged into the middle of a carnal dream. The sun broke through the clouds and warmed her skin, but Natalie hardly noticed when Liam heated her so effortlessly. A tingling, hot feeling of excitement curled in her lower belly. Her rational nature and tight control receded into a misty background under the influence of Liam's hands and mouth. She tangled her fingers in the hair at his nape and then explored the bare skin and corded muscles of his neck.

It thrilled her to feel a shudder run through him at her touch.

Amazing…awesome, even, that she could make such a strong man tremble with just a caress. He was having the same effect on her, causing her to quiver by spreading his big hands over her hips and rubbing her in a slight circular motion, increasing the already taut friction between their straining bodies.

She perfectly felt his arousal but she wasn't offended. It all seemed so natural…so good, despite the newness of the sensation. She gloried in the knowledge that she could evoke such a strong response from him. A hazy fog of sensuality encapsulated her. For a brief, magical moment she knew only the taste of Liam, the feel of him…and the fierce need to experience more.

She was so overwhelmed by the power of Liam's kiss, that it didn't really penetrate her awareness that a car was approaching until Liam pulled away. She opened her eyelids sluggishly, feeling like there was a weight pressing down on them. His face hovered just a few inches above her own. He studied her through a narrow-eyed gaze, his eyes gleaming crescents.

She started when a car door slammed just feet away. A sound of distress leaked out of her throat when she saw Brigit Kavanaugh, Liam's mother, hesitating by her dark blue sedan.

"Liam?" Brigit asked uncertainly.

"Yeah, Ma," Liam replied without removing his gaze from Natalie. How could his voice sound so even? Natalie wondered, disorientated. She jerked her hips and dropped her hands from his shoulders. She'd been holding him as if he was a life preserver and she'd been drowning.

What the hell had just happened?

Liam's mouth flattened and he stepped back.

"I'm sorry…I didn't mean to intrude," Brigit said, sounding contrite. "I brought over the buffer for the floors. I tried to call first, but—"

"It's okay," Liam said gruffly, glancing away from Natalie for the first time since his mother had arrived. Natalie's gaze flickered over Brigit Kavanaugh as embarrassment began to zoom through her veins like a toxin. Her cheeks flamed hot, and she felt slightly dizzy.

She knew who Brigit Kavanaugh was, of course, even though they'd never officially met. Liam's mother was in her late fifties or early sixties, Natalie would have guessed, but she appeared ten years younger. She still had an excellent figure—petite and fit. Her blond hair was styled in a fashionable cut that emphasized Brigit's high cheekbones and a pair of striking cornflower blue eyes. Despite all the cold shoulders Brigit had received from some Harbor Towners when she'd moved here with Liam and Colleen fifteen years ago, she'd managed to win the townspeople over with her hard work on philanthropic projects and her willingness to always help out people in need.

Brigit was the type of woman who commanded attention even from a distance, but she was downright formidable up close. Even though Brigit's glance at her was mild enough, Natalie sensed the power of her personality.

"It's really turned lovely after that rain, hasn't it?" Brigit directed her question toward Natalie with friendly politeness.

She doesn't know who you are, a voice in her head shouted. *If she did, she wouldn't be so civil.*

She recognized that Liam's mother was trying to ease Natalie's discomfort, but Brigit's attempt had the opposite effect, for several reasons, one being that Brigit seemed perfectly comfortable with the idea of coming upon her youngest son while he was making out with a woman. Of course, Brigit had probably witnessed him dallying with countless females since he was old enough to date. Natalie was just another forgetful face in the ongoing stream of women that paraded across the stage of Liam's life.

She'd hired him to do a job. One second, their arrangement had been going fine—professional, if tense—and the next she'd been melting beneath Liam's kiss like a piece of chocolate dropped on the pavement beneath a scalding summer sun.

"Excuse me," Natalie murmured throatily as she threaded her way between Liam's body and her car. She felt Liam's stare tingling on her neck, but she got in her car and shut the door without another word. Casting a furtive glance at Liam and his mother, she turned her vehicle in the circular turnabout and drove off. Brigit looked a little confused, but Liam's face looked fixed and somber. Undoubtedly, he was already regretting that kiss.

Why *had* Liam kissed her? Natalie wondered for the thousandth time as she locked up the office two nights later.

Once again, she was the last one to leave. Out of her two officemates, both attorneys, she was the only single one, and her work habits reflected the fact that she had no one to rush home to at night.

She did a mental eye roll when she realized she was feeling sorry for herself. It was a new thing for her, to mope about her single status or about the fact that she occasionally experienced feelings of acute loneliness. She'd had the recurrent feeling since her mother had died. Natalie didn't like to consider that this mood had settled much more since last Sunday.

Since Liam's kiss.

It was a beautiful August night. The sun had set, but its dusky pink afterglow lingered in the sky over Lake Michigan. Instead of walking to her car, Natalie strolled down Main Street toward the harbor, removing her suit jacket in order to better appreciate the mild breeze coming off the lake.

She had to admit the truth—that kiss had rattled her comfortable world. Natalie wasn't too pleased about that. She'd obviously underestimated her ability to invite Liam Kavanaugh into her organized life and not be shaken up by his dynamic, volatile presence.

Somehow, the memories of how she'd felt under the influence of Liam's coaxing mouth and knowing hands had crowded everything else out of her mind…including the reason she'd hired him. Her obsession to know more about the reasons for Derry Kavanaugh's actions on the night of the crash had faded to the background during the past few days.

The realization made her want to call Liam. Why shouldn't she check in for an update on his investigation? The longer she avoided him, the more it would seem obvious that his kiss had actually been significant.

She was digging in her briefcase for her cell phone when someone shouted her name. She looked across the street, her hand still jammed in her bag. Liam stood in the parking lot of Jake's Place, a popular local restaurant and bar. He waved his hand in a beckoning gesture as she just stared at him for a moment, frozen in surprise at suddenly seeing the object of her chaotic thoughts.

"Hey," he said pleasantly when she crossed the street and approached him. He wore a pair of jeans and an open-collared dark gray shirt. He stood next to a sleek, silver and black motorcycle. Natalie had no doubt it was his. Marc and Liam had both ridden bikes during their high school years; she'd seen Liam countless times ripping down a Harbor Town street with some girl who looked thrilled to be clutching onto him.

"Hi," Natalie replied, hoping that she sounded completely at ease with this unexpected meeting. In truth, her heart had started to beat an erratic tempo against her breastbone.

"I was just going to walk over and see if you were still in your office."

"Were you?"

The lights in the parking lot were dim, but she still saw

something indefinable flicker across his face. "What...you don't believe me?"

"Why wouldn't I believe you?" she asked, glad to hear her voice sounded calm.

He gave her a level look. "Mainly because you sounded like I was full of crap for saying it," she thought she heard him say under his breath. A car door slammed in the distance. Liam glanced past her shoulder and waved at a man who was walking toward them. He continued quietly. "I really was about to walk over to your office, whether you believe me or not. I saw your car parked on Ontario Avenue and figured you were still there. Do you make it a habit to work until almost nine o'clock?"

"Why were you trying to find me?"

Liam scowled when she ignored his question. "I thought you might want to sit in on this conversation. I did a little digging and rumor has it that this guy—" he nodded toward the man he'd just waved at who was approaching where they stood "—saw my father on Silver Dunes Beach on the night of the crash. Not sure yet if it would have been before or after the time period he was at the club. I thought you might be interested," he finished in a low murmur.

"Of course I'm interested, but..." Liam looked up as the man's footsteps grew closer.

"Roger Dayson?" Liam asked.

"That's right." Although Roger's gruff voice was amiable enough, he gave Liam a cautious glance. He was in his late forties and had the weathered complexion of an outdoorsman. He stuck out his hand and Liam shook it. "You must be Liam Kavanaugh."

"As charged. Thanks for stopping by. Like I said on the phone, I got your name and number from Joe Brown. He seemed to think you might have some information about my father's actions on the night of the crash sixteen years ago."

"Not a problem. I usually swing by Jake's on Tuesday nights, so it wasn't out of my way. As for what I saw on the night of the crash, it doesn't amount to much."

"Anything you can tell us will be useful. This is Natalie Reyes. She'll be joining us."

Natalie opened her mouth to protest, but was interrupted by Roger.

"Ma'am," Roger said cordially, extending his hand to her as well.

"Shall we go inside?" Liam suggested.

The two men started toward the door of Jake's Place, but Natalie wavered in her planted heels. As if he'd sensed Natalie hadn't followed, Liam turned around and paused.

"What's wrong?"

She watched as Roger approached the entrance of Jake's Place. Someone exited before he got to the door. Live music and the sound of people having a good time leaked out into the still night air. Jake's was hopping.

"Natalie?" Liam asked, looking puzzled by her hesitancy. "Is everything okay?"

"Of course," she lied. She'd never admit to Liam Kavanaugh, of all people, that she'd never set foot in the popular hangout. Everyone in Harbor Town went to Jake's, whether to enjoy the live music on Tuesday nights, to hang out with friends or to celebrate with family on special occasions.

Everyone but Natalie, that is.

"Come on, then," Liam prompted. He casually grabbed her hand and led her toward the entrance.

She pulled back on his hand, but he refused to let go.

"Wait…let me at least put on my jacket," she said.

His blue eyes skimmed over the ivory, sleeveless silk shell she'd worn under her suit. Her arms were bare. She suddenly felt like she was naked under Liam's stare. "Jacket?" he mumbled, dumbfounded. His gaze lingered for a heartbeat on her breasts before he met hers. "You look fantastic. Why would you want to cover up?"

She was so caught off balance by his compliment that she again didn't utter the protest on her tongue when he started walking toward the door. Natalie couldn't decide what was making her more nervous, the prospect of entering the jam-packed bar or the feeling of Liam's large, warm hand enclosing her own. She began to think it was the latter, because Liam's hold was all she really focused on when they entered the dim interior of Jake's. Thank goodness, or else her anxiety about being in such a public place might have morphed into panic.

The band was in full swing, the singer belting out the refrain from a popular country-rock ballad. Faces swam before her eyes. She was vaguely aware of men and women alike calling out friendly greetings to Liam. An attractive blonde wearing a ruby satin top beneath a tight jean jacket wrapped her hand around his upper arm. To his credit, Liam didn't pause as he moved through the crowd, and his greeting toward the blonde was friendly, but neutral.

Natalie glanced behind her as they passed and saw the woman staring after Liam with a mixture of longing and irritation at his passing. She thought she knew who the woman was—Betsy Darnel. She'd been in the year behind Eric in school. Betsy's gaze sharpened on her, as though she'd just noticed Natalie cowering behind Liam's back.

Roger had already located a booth, apparently only empty because it was too distant to see or hear the band clearly. She slid into the booth, placing her briefcase between herself and the wall. Her breath caught when Liam slid onto the seat next to her and she felt his hip and thigh press against her own. His clean, spicy scent filtered into her nose. She inched toward the wall, trying not to seem too obvious. Liam gave her a sidelong, too-knowing glance and she froze. Their sides were no longer pressed together, but his hard, jeans-covered thigh still ghosted against her leg.

A waitress came and Liam and Roger exchanged some pleasantries until she returned with their drink orders. After the waitress walked away, Liam got down to business.

"I understand from Joe that you were on Silver Dunes Beach on the night of the crash and saw my father," Liam began.

At first, Natalie had been puzzled about Liam's earlier reference to Joe Brown. Natalie knew the gruff old man—he was a Harbor Town old-timer and handyman. He did everything from yard work to simple house repairs to carpentry and painting. Upon reflection, however, she realized it made good sense to use Joe as a reference. Old Joe, as some of the residents fondly referred to him, was an insider to Harbor Town's history, people and secrets. Joe saw and heard a lot of things in his daily meanderings.

"That's right," Roger agreed. "I wasn't a full-time resident of Harbor Town at the time. I'd come down with some buddies for some R and R and some fishing in Miller Lake," he said.

"You were staying in one of those vacation cottages near Silver Dune Beach?" Liam clarified.

Roger nodded his gray head and took a swig of his beer. "There's a path that leads from the cottages to the beach, but you can take another branch off the path toward Miller Lake. I'd left the cottage around sunset and gone down to the lake…" Roger paused and cast an uncertain glance at Liam from beneath shaggy eyebrows.

"I'm not the police chief yet," Liam said mildly. Unlike Natalie, Roger seemed to understand Liam perfectly, because he gave a booming bark of laughter and relaxed back in his seat.

"Ernie Prang—he was the chief back then—didn't take too kindly to trapping in Miller Lake," Roger said slyly.

"I know," Liam said. "He always said it was unsportsmanlike."

"How do you stand on the matter?" Roger asked, his pale eyes sparkling with mischief.

"I stand where the law does," Liam replied.

"In other words, I better not be caught laying fish traps when you get sworn into office."

Liam's shrug and easy smile looked casual enough, but Natalie got the impression Roger Dayson would definitely think twice about putting illegal fish traps into Miller Lake once Liam was the face of the law in Harbor County.

"Like I said, I haven't been sworn into office yet. But I'd *like* to think I'll have better things to do with my time once I am chief then to crack down on a sixteen-year-old misdemeanor," Liam said dryly. "So please…go on with your story."

"Well it was after sunset by the time I headed back to the cabin. It was a full moon that night, so I took a detour to the beach to get a good look at it. That's when I saw your father."

"How long after sunset was it?" Liam asked.

Roger shrugged and his eyebrows pinched together. "Couldn't have been much more than twenty minutes or so after dark."

"Was there anyone else on the beach but my father?"

Roger shook his head. "Just me and your dad."

"And?" Liam prompted when Roger clammed up and took a long drink of his beer. "Did you two speak?"

"No…not really," said Roger, suddenly seeming uncomfortable.

"What happened?" Liam persisted.

Roger's glance at Liam was a bit anxious. "Your dad…he was real upset."

"How do you know?"

The man made a sheepish motion with his head. "He was crying."

"Crying?" Liam repeated in a deadpan tone. Natalie examined his profile. His facial features remained unreadable, but she sensed he was stunned by Roger's words.

"Yeah," Roger admitted. "I've never really…heard anything like that before. Your dad…he was a big man. You have the look of him, so you must know what I mean," he said with a significant nod toward Liam. "It just took me by surprise to come upon a man like that so obviously upset. He didn't take too well to me seeing him, either. When he noticed I was on the beach with him, he looked like he was going to tear me to pieces for intruding on such a…you know…private moment. I'm not going to lie to you, I got off that beach like a fire had been lit under me."

Liam just stared.

"Did he seem intoxicated?" Natalie asked, covering for Liam's apparent shocked state.

Roger shrugged uncertainly. "Maybe. Mostly he seemed like someone had just told him his best friend had been killed. He looked like a mess, you know?"

"And you two never actually spoke?" Natalie prompted Roger.

"Nope. It left an impression on me though. To this day, in my mind's eye I can just see him standing alone on that beach. He was the picture of misery. I felt terrible for interrupting him," Roger mumbled glumly before he took another swig of his beer.

Liam straightened slowly, seeming to rise out of his thoughts.

"The crash happened about a half hour after you saw him, I'm guessing, given what you said about sunset. Isn't that right?" Liam asked, looking to her for confirmation.

Natalie nodded.

A strange expression came over Roger's face. Natalie saw him studying her glasses and the uncovered scarring on her temple as if he was seeing her for the first time.

"You were actually *in* that crash. You were that little girl," he said in a hushed tone.

"Yes. I was in the car with my mother."

"Damn," Roger muttered under his breath. He threw Liam a wary glance and then looked back at Natalie. "If I'd known Derry Kavanaugh was…you know…in such a bad way drink-wise, I might have done something to stop him from getting into a car, but I *swear,* I didn't guess he was intoxicated."

"Of course you would have done something if you'd known," Natalie reassured quickly.

"Is there anything else you can remember?" Liam asked. She had the feeling he was trying to deflect Roger from staring at her face with so much distress and fascination.

Roger shook his head. "Sorry. Nothing else."

"Did you see my father leave?" Liam asked.

"No. Like I said, I hightailed it off the beach when your dad turned around and glared at me like he was going to take my head off."

"And you didn't know he was Derry Kavanaugh until later?"

"No, not until I saw his photo in the papers after the crash and put two and two together," Roger replied, giving Natalie another furtive glance. He shifted uneasily in his seat.

"Listen…if that's all…" Roger faded off and waved vaguely in the direction of the crowd and the band.

"It is. I can't thank you enough for agreeing to speak with us," Liam said. He stood along with Roger and shook his hand. Roger nodded at Natalie politely as he took his leave, but she had the impression he was glad to make his escape.

Liam slid back into his seat directly next to her. She tensed. Wouldn't it have been more natural for him to sit across from her since Roger had left? And was it her imagination, or had he pressed closer to the side of her body this time?

"Well, that was interesting," Liam said.

She studied his profile and wondered what he was thinking. Surely it hadn't been easy for him to hear what Roger had said. Regret trickled into her awareness.

"You seemed surprised," Natalie murmured, her voice barely audible above the raucous music of the band. "You don't have any idea why your father was so upset?"

"Not a clue," Liam said.

"Your...your mother never mentioned any reason why he might have been in such a state on that night?"

He turned. His eyes were a dark, cobalt blue in the dim light as they flicked over her. He shook his head.

"I'll tell you one thing, though," he said.

She leaned toward him.

"I never saw my father cry a tear in his life. Never."

For a moment, neither of them spoke.

"Something happened to him that night," Natalie whispered.

"Something," Liam muttered in agreement. He transferred his gaze to the empty seat across from them as his thigh shifted beneath the table, brushing her skirt against her thigh. "Maybe the video from the bar will tell me something more about what happened to my dad that night."

"So you haven't seen it yet?"

"No. I'm scheduled to go to the police headquarters Thursday morning. A friend of mine is going to get the video out of storage."

Natalie was quiet for a moment. "Has your mother ever spoken to you about the last time she saw your dad?"

Liam shook his head. "The only thing she ever told us is that he came back from Chicago earlier than she'd expected. He usually stayed in the city from Monday to Thursday night and joined us at the vacation house for a long weekend during the summer months."

"The crash happened on a Tuesday night," Natalie recalled. "And your mother never said why she thought he showed up unexpectedly?"

"No. Like I've told you before, we don't make a habit of standing around at family barbecues, reminiscing about the crash."

She recoiled slightly at the hard edge to his voice. He must have noticed, because he sighed and slumped back in the booth. His thigh pressed tighter against hers, but Natalie doubted he noticed. He seemed so deflated.

"Sorry for snapping at you," he mumbled. He started to flip a spoon that had been sitting on the table between his long, agile fingers.

"It's okay," she said, meaning it. She recalled what Roger Dayson had said about Derry Kavanaugh on the beach.

He seemed like someone had just told him his best friend had been killed.

"I know this can't be easy for you," she said quietly as she watched the movement of his fingers.

"I'm sure it's not a picnic in the park for you, either."

She glanced up, surprised because his low, gruff voice sounded closer to her ear than she'd expected. His goatee looked so trim and sleek up close. It highlighted his firm mouth to perfection. The thought of what those whiskers would feel like beneath her fingertips rose in her mind to taunt her. She still could hear the rowdy music in the distance, so she couldn't explain why it suddenly felt as if the two of them were encapsulated in an airtight bubble.

"Are you sure you want to do this, Natalie?"

"Yes. Are you regretting it? Taking the job, I mean?"

His expression remained impassive, but his eyes seemed warm as they flickered across her face.

"I don't regret it enough to make me stop doing it."

She just nodded, unable to glance away.

"I wish you'd take off those glasses."

"What?" she asked, knocked off balance by his abrupt statement.

"I can't see your eyes. It's dark back here." His low, gruff murmur mesmerized her, even though she should have been alarmed by the fact that his firm mouth had just lowered another inch toward her lips. "Go ahead, Natalie. Take them off. I want to look at you."

Chapter Five

When she remained frozen, a small smile tilted his lips. The spoon thumped to the wood table. He reached with both hands and gently drew off her glasses.

"There. That's better," he said as he placed her glasses on the table. "You okay?"

She blinked. Thankfully, her eyelid didn't quiver or droop. Liam had been right. The light back here in the alcove was indeed dim enough for comfort. She nodded, despite the fact that her heart had started to hammer out a warning in her ears. She wasn't used to having anyone staring at her as frankly—as warmly—as Liam Kavanaugh was at the moment.

"It makes you uncomfortable, when people look at you," he said, making her wonder if he was a mind reader.

"If you'd had people gaping at you like you were a freak since you were eleven years old, you might not adore the experience, either," she said stiffly. She turned away, wishing that her scars faced the wall and not Liam's sharp eyes. The scoffing noise he made caused her to whip her chin around, though.

"Sorry." He must have noticed her insulted expression. "But come on...no one is looking at you like you're a freak. That's just stupid."

Anger rose in her, swift and fierce. "What do *you* know about it?" How could he, a man who had probably never known self-consciousness once in his entire life, stand in judgment of her experience? "You saw the way Roger Dayson stared at me once he realized who I was."

"I'm sure he was curious once he figured out who you were, but that's not why most people are staring at you."

She gaped at him, incredulous at his confidence. He noticed and shook his head. Natalie got the impression he really did consider her something of a bizarre novelty.

"They're looking at you because you're beautiful," he said, his brows cocked, his manner saying loud and clear he was telling her the obvious...like, *hello*.

She made a scoffing sound. When his expression remained earnest, if puzzled, she sighed.

"What difference does it make?" she asked irritably.

He leaned closer, so that when he spoke she felt his breath brush against her temple.

"It makes a difference to me," he said. "It should to you. Natalie?"

"Yes," she mouthed.

"I wish it made a difference to you."

She looked up at him slowly. Sure enough, his mouth hovered just inches away from her own. He'd moved closer. Her left arm lay flush against his torso. The tingling tip of her left breast pressed against his ribs.

His mouth lowered, and Natalie realized distantly she'd entered that fog of sensuality that had encapsulated her several days ago in Liam's driveway. Despite her heart pumping out a warning, she couldn't seem to gather sufficient will to do much of anything but anticipate Liam's mouth closing on her own.

A man spoke and a woman laughed shrilly. Natalie started and saw two men and a blonde woman walking toward the booth in front of them. She recognized Betsy Darnel. Betsy had taken off her jacket. Her top looked more like a draped silk handkerchief tied around her neck than a blouse. It covered her chest, but left her shoulders, back and a strip of belly almost completely bare. The two men who had accompanied her to the table were shamelessly checking out Betsy's rearview as she came toward their booth, but Betsy only had eyes for Liam.

"Hi, Liam," Betsy said.

"Hey, Betsy."

"Let me out. Please," Natalie hissed quietly.

"When I saw you at the Shop and Save yesterday you said you were too busy to come to Jake's tonight," Betsy reminded Liam, unaware of Natalie's mutterings. Natalie put her glasses back on and grabbed her bag. Her need to get out of the crowded bar had just grown exponentially. "I guess you changed your mind about coming," Betsy continued, sounding a little sulky. "How come you're sitting way back here, where you can't even hear the music very well?"

"We were talking. We needed some quiet. And some privacy," Liam replied. Natalie shoved her bag into his ribs, making him grunt.

"Talking, huh?" Betsy mused. Liam gave Natalie a surprised, annoyed glance and scooted out of the seat, probably because he didn't want to be jabbed again. Once Natalie's way was clear she shot out of the booth as if she'd been stored under pressure. "I hope I'm not interrupting a personal moment or anything," Betsy said as she gave Natalie the once-over.

Natalie hitched her bag onto her shoulder, highly aware of Liam's tall form hovering over her the whole time.

"No, nothing personal," she told Betsy coolly. "It was just a business meeting. Good night."

She ignored Betsy's sarcastic laugh of disbelief.

"Natalie, wait."

She heard Liam call out, but she ignored him as she rushed away.

Brigit Kavanaugh waved distractedly at Liam from her kneeling position in her garden.

"Something is eating my lettuce and tomatoes, Chief. I demand answers!" she said with mock imperiousness as she stood.

"If you're implying my soon-to-be job is going to involve hot pursuits of salad-eating rabbits, you're not doing much to bolster my confidence about taking it."

Liam felt a little guilty, given his reason for being there, when his mother laughed in a carefree manner. She didn't laugh enough, nowadays.

"That sun is fierce. Come on, let's go in the air-conditioning. I want to talk to you about something," Liam said.

Brigit led him into the cool, shaded front room. The Kavanaughs hardly ever used the living room. They were a kitchen, front porch or beach sort of family. There had been a formal dining room and an elegant parlor in Liam's childhood home in Chicago; he didn't miss them a bit. Even before the lawsuits, even before they'd moved to the Harbor Town vacation home permanently, the Kavanaughs hadn't spent much time in stuffy surroundings. His brother and sisters had always begged to eat in the kitchen or on their large, shaded terrace; most nights they'd been indulged. Derry Kavanaugh had made the kind of salary that allowed him to support his wife's tastes in luxury, but Derry himself would rather eat in the cozy, slightly messy kitchen with his children than in the formal dining room.

"So what's this all about?" Brigit asked briskly as she sat next to him on the tufted couch.

Liam didn't know how to start. It was more difficult than he'd anticipated, broaching the topic of his father. In the end, he just took the plunge. "Mom, was Dad upset when you saw him? On the night of the accident?"

Brigit's smile shrunk.

"What?" she croaked, her expression leading Liam to believe she wasn't quite sure she'd heard him correctly.

"On the night of the accident. Was Dad upset? You saw him before he went out, isn't that right?"

"Why are you asking about this all of a sudden?"

He grimaced when he heard the offended, stiff quality of her voice. "I'm sorry, Ma, I don't want to upset you, but it's something I've been wondering about."

"Why? It happened sixteen years ago. Why should it matter now?"

He considered his mother's face in the dim light. He couldn't help but recall that she'd had a heart attack a year ago. It had been a mild one, granted, and Brigit currently was a picture of health. Still…the thought hovered over him like a dark, threatening cloud.

"I'm investigating the events that led up to the crash," he said quietly.

The silence seemed to swell and billow.

"I don't understand, Liam."

Her bewildered expression pained him. He wanted the truth. But at what cost was he willing to get it?

He picked up his mother's hand, trying to reassure her.

"Someone has hired me to find out any information I can about why Dad behaved so uncharacteristically that night."

"Someone *hired* you?" Brigit regarded him like a stranger who had suddenly sat beside her speaking a foreign language. "Who on earth would *want* to hire you—"

He saw the moment when she guessed at the truth. Her face settled into a cold, grim mask.

"Of course. The only person who would want to hire you for such a ridiculous task would be someone who was involved. That woman I saw you with the other day at your house...the one wearing the dark glasses. That was the Reyes girl, wasn't it?" she asked.

"Natalie Reyes. Yeah."

"I see," Brigit said coldly. She removed her hand from his.

"I don't think you do at all," Liam said slowly.

Brigit's sharp blue eyes flashed to meet his. "Don't I? She's a very pretty girl."

Liam attempted to bury his anger at the insult, knowing his mother had cause to be upset. "I didn't accept the assignment because she's *pretty*."

"She's paying you a good sum, then?"

"I didn't accept it for the money, either," he shot back. "As a matter of fact, I'm going to return the money this evening. I want to do this for me, Mom. For us. For Marc and Deidre and Colleen...for Dad. Doesn't he deserve to have someone try to understand him? Everyone has painted him as such a selfish bastard over the years. Is it really so strange I would want to get a more realistic picture of the man who caused that crash...a more *human* picture?"

"Selfish bastard?" Brigit repeated. Liam noticed her lips had gone white at the corners and she moved them as though they were numb. "That's how you've been seeing your father?"

"No! Of course not. I'm just saying, most people would look at the situation from the outside and—"

Brigit stood up abruptly, halting him. "I'm not going to say anything more about this, Liam," she told him in a low, shaking voice that set off alarms in his head. "I can't tell you how disappointed I am in you at this moment, that you would consider doing something so disrespectful of your father's memory. All for a girl."

Liam sprung up from the couch, his worries about his mother's well-being evaporating beneath the cold sarcasm of her tone.

"I'm not doing it for a girl. I'm doing it for the truth. I'd think you'd want that as well, Mom, but maybe I'm seeing things a little clearer now. You're pretty damn happy leaving everything locked up tight, aren't you? That suits you just fine."

She walked out of the room. A few seconds later, he heard her rapid footsteps on the stairs.

Guilt ripped through him when he recalled her incredulous, hurt expression.

Natalie had a sneaking suspicion who was visiting when she heard the brisk, authoritative knock the following evening, just before the door opened.

"Let's get one thing straight. I kissed you first the other day, but you sure as hell kissed me back."

Natalie sat at her desk, stunned into complete silence not only by the first words that flew out of Liam's mouth, but the unexpected sight of him standing in her office. He wore a white long-sleeved cotton shirt with the unbuttoned cuffs rolled back once and a scowl on his face. His short, golden-brown hair was mussed, as if he'd been raking his fingers through it in frustration.

What in the world was he talking about? Natalie loosened

fingers that had gone stiff in the last few seconds and set her pen on the blotter.

"Well good evening to you, too," she murmured calmly.

He gave her an irritated glance and fell into the leather chair in front of her desk like a dead weight.

"That's just great, that's priceless," he muttered. "It's so... *you,* to say something like that. That response proves my point completely."

"And what point would that be?" she asked, strangely not at all offended by his behavior. If anything, she was a little concerned by his distracted, agitated manner.

"It means just what I said. That's just the kind of thing you'd say to something inflammatory. *Well good evening to you, too.* Or what about, *no, nothing personal, it was just a business meeting.*" He shook his head as though he was exhausted by her antics, but his eyes studied her with a sharp gleam. "If that's the way you kiss all your business associates it's a wonder you aren't the most popular accountant on the planet."

The mention of that kiss finally pricked her anger, which is what he'd intended all along.

"How dare you barge in here and say something like that to me," she said as she began to straighten the papers on her desk.

"I'd dare a hell of a lot more."

She paused in her paper shuffling and glanced at him. He looked as lazy and uncaring as a big cat stretching in the hot summer sun. The analogy was completely apt. A big cat could turn dangerous in a heartbeat.

It took her a second to realize she'd stood up in her mounting fury and confusion.

"We *do* have a business arrangement. I was just stating the truth last night," she said, her voice quavering.

"We kissed, and it was good. *Really* good. Now *I'm* just stating the truth, Natalie."

She halted the retort on her tongue at the last second. She studied him more closely, noticing the tension in his muscles that belied his lazy pose. "What's happened? What's gotten into you? You didn't come here to talk to me about…*that*," she said, not wanting to utter the word *kiss*.

At first, he didn't reply or move, but then his lean body uncoiled from his sitting position. He stuck one hand into a back pocket of his jeans.

Natalie stared at the folded piece of paper he tossed on her desk. She felt sick. She didn't need to open it to know it was the check she'd written him for a retainer.

"My mother seems to be of the opinion that the reason I took this case is because I find you so attractive," he said.

"You…you told your mother I hired you?" she asked, her queasiness mounting.

"I went to try and ask her about my dad's behavior on the night of the crash. She's not very happy with me at the moment."

Compassion swelled in her breast. No wonder he seemed so out of sorts.

"I've been thinking about this situation all afternoon, and you know what I decided, Natalie?" He pointed at the check on her desk. "*That* was making things more complicated. Not me kissing you."

She glanced up at him cautiously. He looked a little fearsome in that moment, his face tight and eyes blazing.

"What do you mean?"

"Maybe you were right for calling it business last night. You paying me made this a *business* arrangement, just like you said. So you can keep your money."

Yes. Of course he was right, Natalie told herself. She quashed down her intense disappointment at the thought of

Liam changing his mind about the investigation and forced herself to breathe evenly.

"I understand," she said.

"No you don't."

She gaped at him as he continued.

"See, my mother was right, too. A little. I didn't take the case just because I find you attractive, but it might have been a contributing factor."

"I don't believe that. You took the case because your gut told you it was the right thing to do."

He didn't reply for a moment, but just stared at her with stormy eyes.

"I agree, in essence," he eventually said gruffly. "That's why I came here, to tell you I'm completing the investigation to the best of my ability, but not for money."

"But—"

He pointed at her. "If you think I'm going to walk away now when I'm just starting to get a picture of what was happening with my dad on that night, you're dead wrong. And I've got a hell of a lot more resources than any other investigator you could hire, so you're not going to get rid of me unless you've decided you don't care anymore about what happened on that night."

"Of course I still care!"

"Fine. Then we can do this as partners. We're two people with a common history who are looking into events that led up to a mutual family tragedy. See, this *is* personal to me, Natalie. Nobody can put something this personal on ice."

He started for the door. "Liam...wait," she said desperately. He paused and glanced around. Was it her imagination, or did she see a trace of regret on his face? "So you're...you're definitely going to continue with the investigation?"

He nodded solemnly. "I'm going to watch the tape at state

police headquarters tomorrow. Why don't I stop by your house afterward, around seven o'clock?"

"Stop by my house..."

He started to walk out the door again, making her fade off. "Yeah. I'll take you out to dinner and tell you what I saw on the tape." He opened the door and glanced back at her. "Just two single, consenting adults enjoying each other's company and discussing matters of a highly personal nature. Can't get any simpler than that, right?"

He closed the door quietly behind him. The only comfort she could take from the volatile meeting was that given Liam's ironic tone as he took his leave, he obviously agreed with her that the situation was the polar opposite of simple.

His friend Derek Oberman was nice enough to set him up with a TV, VCR and an empty conference room at the state police headquarters in Lansing. He knew Derek from his early days on the Chicago Police Department when they'd both worked west-side patrol.

Derek lingered as Liam turned on the television and prepared the tape.

"Do you want me to stay and watch it with you?" Derek asked a little awkwardly as a gray-and-white image of what was undoubtedly the Silver Dunes bar flickered onto the screen. Liam paused the tape and turned to his friend.

"Nah, you better go and look busy or your captain will catch onto you letting me in here. You'll be getting a midnight tan before you know it," Liam joked, referring to one of a police officer's least preferred duties—night patrol.

Derek laughed, but looked a little relieved at Liam's pardon as he started to back out of the room. "You want anything to eat? We've got some leftover doughnuts from the morning briefing."

"No need," Liam said with a grin. The last thing he wanted

to do at that moment was eat, as nervous as he felt about watching the tape. After Derek had gone, he sat down at the conference table and clicked the play button on the VCR.

He fast-forwarded through several hours of surveillance tape until he finally saw the familiar head and shoulders appear at the bottom of the screen. His heart leaping into his throat, he rewound and hit Play again.

He'd forgotten the power of his father's presence. The camera was placed at an angle that showed Derry Kavanaugh's back as he sat at the bar with two men and one other woman. Liam knew that the Silver Dunes Country Club was typically crowded from Thursdays through Sundays, but this had clearly been a slow Tuesday. With no weekend sports to entertain the crowd, the television mounted behind the gleaming walnut wood bar was tuned to the news.

Derry sat a good distance away from the other people, his shoulders hunched slightly. Jack Andreason, the bartender, smiled jovially as he greeted Derry. Liam suspected Jack had served his dad many times in the past and that he was used to bantering with Derry about sports or politics. It didn't seem to take Jack long to catch onto Derry's mood, however. Although Liam couldn't see his father's face, he saw how Jack's smile sagged after two seconds of interacting with his father. He brought Derry his drink and walked away to clean some glasses. Liam guessed from the dark color of his father's drink that he was drinking whiskey neat.

It felt as if he'd been plugged into a low-grade electrical outlet when Liam noticed his father's wedding ring on his right hand. His father jiggled the gold circlet with his thumb in a nervous, edgy gesture before he reached for his glass of disappearing whiskey.

Liam watched the entire period Derry was there—one hour, twenty-seven minutes and thirteen seconds of spying on the last moments of his father's life. The longer Derry sat there, the more a pressure intensified in Liam's chest. It was ludicrous, and he knew it, but he wished like hell he could reach through the television screen and somehow force his father not to leave that bar.

The man he watched was obviously miserable, but things would have looked better in the morning. Things were *always* better, come morning.

But his dad never saw another dawn.

The moment came, of course, just as Liam knew it would. Derry stood and threw some cash on the bar. Liam searched hungrily for a glimpse of his face, but he only caught Derry's bold profile before he walked out of the frame and disappeared.

Liam sat for a full five minutes, eyes closed, his hand covering his lower face, unmoving.

Then he rewound the tape and watched the entire sequence again…and again.

She felt ridiculous for taking so much time with her appearance, but her anxiety over the matter couldn't overpower a desire to look as good as possible. She glanced at the clock she kept on her bathroom counter.

It's not a date, for goodness' sake, she mentally chastised herself as she fastened her earring. He'd never said it was. They were just going to discuss what he'd observed on the surveillance tape.

The only problem was, Liam had made a point of saying their partnership in uncovering the truths from their past was *not* a business venture, either.

He'd told her point-blank he was attracted to her.

She really shouldn't have allowed him to burst into her office and dictate terms the way he had. She'd told herself repeatedly over the past twenty-four hours that the only reason she hadn't called him and told him not to come tonight was that part of her believed he was right. It was ridiculous to say this venture was anything but—

"Personal," Natalie whispered to herself as she stood in front of the bathroom mirror. Something fluttered in her stomach hearing that word.

But just *how* personal did Liam Kavanaugh mean? That was the question that kept haunting her.

She hadn't been sure what to wear. What if she looked too dressy and Liam showed up in shorts and a T-shirt? She'd compromised with a pair of jeans, some high-heeled leather sandals and a jade-green knit halter top.

She picked up a comb and stroked her hair. Her extra efforts had paid off. The dark chestnut strands tumbled in loose curls all the way to her waist. She'd spent an extra five minutes moisturizing her skin. Her bare shoulders gleamed in the bathroom light.

She hesitated when she picked up her glasses, tempted to leave them behind, then almost dropped them in the sink when she heard the doorbell.

"Hi," she said when she opened the front door, her voice cracking from nerves.

"Hi."

He'd dressed for dinner. Not formally by any means—Natalie just couldn't picture a guy like Liam putting on a suit for dinner—but he'd made an effort with his appearance, nonetheless. Not that he needed to. The result left her speechless.

"Your hair…it's down," he said. The tinge of wonder and warmth in his voice only added to her tongue-tied state.

"You've seen it down before."

"Not in the light," he corrected.

"Please, come in," she muttered, unsure how to respond.

"I like your place," he said as he stepped into her living room. The light in her house was usually muted, due to her eyes' sensitivity. Her town house was homey, though, despite the dimness, thanks to warm colors, sensual fabrics and glowing, ambient light from well-placed lamps. Natalie considered the room proportions in her town house to be quite generous, but Liam made them shrink with his presence.

"Thanks," Natalie said as she watched his gaze travel across every detail of her living room. She got the impression he didn't miss much with those cop's eyes of his.

"You look fantastic," he said.

"So do you."

Her cheeks burned when she realized what she'd just said without even a millisecond of hesitation. When would she learn to think before she spoke? Maybe at the same time she taught herself not to blush at inopportune moments.

"Would you like a quick tour? There's not much to see, but—"

"Lead the way," he said. She showed him the dining room, kitchen and patio, and a few minutes later led him back to the living room.

"You're multitalented," he said. "You dance like a professional and you could have been an interior designer as well. I should get your advice on the cottage."

"It looked like you were doing a great job on your own," Natalie said as she grabbed a light sweater from the entryway and they walked out the door.

Liam shrugged. He checked her lock and closed the door firmly behind him. "I do okay with the basics, but when it comes to colors or arranging furniture, I'm your basic caveman."

"At least you're man enough to admit it."

Liam glanced over at her sharply, grinning when he saw her small smile.

"You didn't bring your bike?" Natalie observed as they approached his sedan.

"No. Disappointed?" he asked as he opened the passenger door for her.

"Very," Natalie replied, looking at him over her shoulder. Perhaps it was foolish of her, but part of her had always envied all those girls she used to see on the back of his motorcycle.

She pulled up short when he reached beneath the fall of her long hair and grasped her upper arm.

"Be careful, Natalie."

His low, rough voice made her shudder.

"What do you mean?"

"If you can't decide if you're innocent or a seductress," he said, leaning closer, "I might have to help you choose."

Chapter Six

She stood motionless, highly aware of him. She felt it when his fingers closed around her long hair. His nostrils flared.

"I don't know what you're talking about," she said. His fist opened, granting her freedom, and she heard his low chuckle.

He shut the passenger door once she was seated.

She made a mental effort to smoothe her choppy breath. Why did it happen so often, that she said something to him in such an off-the-cuff manner, as if she was a practiced flirt? Her occasional responses surprised her, probably more than they did Liam. They just seemed to spill out of her, contrary to her nervousness.

Contrary to her typical desire for control.

Her voice *had* sounded husky there by the car…downright suggestive if the flame that had leaped into Liam's eyes and his ensuing reaction were any indication.

A half hour later, Natalie was heartened to realize she was feeling more comfortable, despite Liam's earlier challenge and her anxious curiosity about his experience at the state police headquarters today.

He'd probably have forgotten the moment by tomorrow, Natalie thought with a mental eye roll.

He'd chosen the Lakeview—a sedate, upscale eatery located in nearby Antioch, Michigan. The Lakeview was one of the few places in the area where Natalie enjoyed dining. The secluded tables and darkened interior afforded her the measure of privacy she preferred. They exchanged little conversation as they examined the menus and then placed their orders.

"You like the place all right?" Liam observed as he watched her gazing out the window onto the brilliant view of the sun setting above the blue waters of Lake Michigan.

She furtively removed her glasses. Although it was Thursday—usually a busy night for the Lakeview—the crowd tonight was thin. She nodded toward the window. "I've lived in this area my whole life, and I never get tired of the sunsets."

"Me, either," Liam agreed.

"And, yes, you're right. This is one of my favorite restaurants." She stared back out at the view, glad that with Liam sitting across from her, she could at least show him the "good" side of her face.

"So I'd heard."

She turned her head. "From whom?"

Liam's shrug looked a little sheepish. "I asked Mari if there was any place she knew you liked. After making such a big deal of things in your office last night, I didn't want to risk taking you to a place like Jake's and having you hate it."

Natalie stared at him, her lips parted. She'd assumed he hadn't noticed her discomfort for what it was the other night.

She'd assumed wrong.

It both pleased and confused her at once that he'd taken the time to ask his sister-in-law about where she might like to dine. Maybe Liam truly did consider their outing as a date of sorts.

"I had dinner with your brother, Marc, and Mari here last fall," Natalie said, thinking it was best to sidestep the issue of her discomfort with crowds and staring eyes.

"Yeah. Mari told me. She said Eric came, too."

"That's right. Marc and Eric even managed not to get into a fight the whole time. All the more reason for me to adore this place."

He gave her a dry glance, and she chuckled.

She examined him closely in the seconds that followed, trying to gauge his mood. He looked wonderful to her in the light of flickering candles and the setting sun. He wore a white button-down shirt with blue stripes, the cuffs open and rolled casually back, revealing his strong, tanned forearms. His eyes seemed to glow in the ambient light as he returned her stare levelly.

His expression sobered.

"So…feuding families aside, I guess you're wondering how things went this afternoon."

"I am curious." Her throat felt tight when she swallowed. She glanced out at the golden pink sky and dark blue lake. "I'm…concerned, as well."

"About what?"

"About you." She kept her gaze on the stunning sunset.

He didn't respond immediately. "I'm touched."

She gave him a sidelong look. "Don't be. Anyone would be worried about you going and watching that tape on your own."

"I told you before, I'm only concerned about what you think."

She rolled her eyes. He laughed softly, but for the first time that evening, she sensed his tension. He played the role of the easygoing, gorgeous daredevil so effortlessly, it was hard for her to see below the surface sometimes.

"I watched the video," he said.

"And?" Natalie prompted hesitantly.

"It wasn't easy."

"No, I'm sure it wasn't."

He circled his iced-tea spoon in his glass several times, removed it and tossed it on a napkin. "It was easy to see why Jack Andreason described my dad as 'sullen' during the trial. I could only see him from the back, but his posture was deflated and wired at once. Jack's good mood seemed to fade when he approached my dad. I wonder what my father said to him."

"There was no sound?"

Liam shook his head. "It's illegal to audiotape someone without their consent."

"I hadn't realized that," Natalie said, disappointed. "You must not have been able to get much from the viewing, then. Did Derry talk to anyone while he was there?"

"No, aside from his interactions with Jack, which were brief. Jack seemed all too happy to keep clear of him."

"So…it wasn't helpful." Regret flooded her, not because the tape was a dead end, but because Liam had risked so much by watching the last hours of his father's life and they weren't any closer to understanding Derry's actions on the night of the crash.

"I wouldn't say it wasn't helpful," Liam replied in a flat tone.

She glanced over at him in surprise, but had to quiet her curiosity when the waiter came with their salads.

"What did you notice?" Natalie asked as soon as the waiter had departed.

"I don't know if it means anything or not, but at one point, my dad snapped at Jack when he tried to change the channel on the television. I couldn't hear anything, but Jack's alarmed look at my dad when he reached for the remote clued me in."

He must have noticed her confused expression.

"There was a television behind the bar. I could see it better than my dad's face. It was mounted above the cash register," Liam explained before he took a bite of his salad.

"I see," she murmured. "So your father was watching something on the television, and he didn't want Jack to change the channel? What was the program?"

"The news," Liam said. He seemed distracted as he put down his fork and pushed his salad away.

"Do you think whatever was on the news is actually relevant?" Natalie asked.

"I don't see how it could be," Liam admitted. "The TV was on CNN, airing a story about a corporate takeover by DuBois Enterprises. Those happen often enough. DuBois seems to gobble up some new company every week. Lincoln DuBois himself was on the screen. I can't imagine why my dad would have barked at Jack that he wanted to watch it. It was definitely because of that story, though, because he wasn't staring at the television before it aired, and he hardly glanced at it again after the clip was over. He left about five minutes after the end of the segment...once he'd finished his drink," Liam finished grimly.

"Isn't DuBois a media conglomerate?"

Liam nodded. "Yeah. A lot more than media is under the DuBois umbrella, though, everything from computer software production, to copper mining, to newspapers and magazines."

Natalie shook her head in confusion and swallowed a final bite of her own salad before she set down her fork. "Did it say who DuBois Enterprises had acquired in the takeover?"

Liam shrugged. "Yeah, I could see the headlines at the

bottom pretty damn well. Some French company called Alerveret that manufactured computer chips."

"Why would your father be interested in that?" Natalie asked as the waiter returned to clear their salad plates. Liam didn't speak until they were alone again.

"Hell if I know. Maybe he wasn't interested in the news story at all. Maybe he was just in a bad mood, and taking it out on Jack."

Natalie considered this possibility as their entrees were served. Liam seemed thoughtful, too. In the distance, she heard the tinkling sounds of a piano.

"I'll go over to the library tomorrow and see if I can't dig up any information on the DuBois takeover of Alerveret. I couldn't find much online," he said.

"Do you think your father could have had investments in Alerveret? Maybe he lost a chunk of money, and that's what upset him."

Liam shook his head dismissively. "He was upset *before* he saw the news clip, remember? Although he seemed damn interested in that story, and even more agitated after he watched it. As far as the bad investment, I think my mom would have told us about that. I never heard her mention losing a huge chunk of money—not *before* the lawsuits, anyway."

Natalie's cheeks heated and she lowered her gaze. The Kavanaughs' socioeconomic status had drastically changed after the lawsuits against Derry Kavanaugh's estate. All that money had gone to Mari and Ryan Itani and Natalie and her brother. The bulk of the money awarded to the Reyes family had paid for Natalie's medical care following the accident. Eric and Natalie had used the remainder to get good educations, something their mother would have wished for them more than anything if she'd lived.

She could tell by his thoughtful manner Liam hadn't meant his comment as a jab. He was just stating a simple fact.

"I'll be sure to check about the direction of Alerveret's stock after DuBois acquired them, though, just to make sure," Liam said.

"Liam?"

He glanced up in the process of cutting his chicken.

"Both Roger Dayson and Jack Andreason seemed to be intimidated by your father on that night. But I'm getting the impression from you that your father wasn't an angry person by nature. Is that correct?"

"I can only remember him getting mad once in my entire childhood. It was the year before he died. I played football in high school, and I had this overzealous coach my freshman year who got aggressive at times. You know the type—dude put his entire identity into leading a bunch of skinny fourteen-year-olds into battle. Anyway, he got a little rough one afternoon practice with one of my friends on the team. My father had shown up unexpectedly to watch me practice, and he saw the whole thing. When Coach ended practice and told us to go shower, my dad barked at him to stay behind. Said he wanted a word. I'd never seen my dad look like that before. He looked like he was going to chew up Coach Bragg and spit him out."

"What happened?" Natalie wondered.

"I wanted to know that myself, so I took an awful slow walk to the locker room. My dad reamed Bragg out. Nothing physical happened, but it seemed to come close to blows a few times." Liam shook his head as if to clear it. "I never saw my coach the same way after that. I used to be intimidated by him, but the memory of how scared he looked while my dad let him have it changed that forever. He never got rough with any of us kids again. I can only imagine what my father threatened him with, if he did. Legal action, probably."

"You remember it so well. It must have made a big impact on you."

"I'm thinking Coach Bragg remembers it a hell of a lot better than me," Liam said wryly before he ate a slice of roasted potato.

"I can imagine. Your father seems bigger than life."

"He made friends wherever he went. My mom used to say he could have charmed the devil into doing good deeds."

Natalie smiled as she buttered a steaming roll. "Sounds like a true Irishman."

Liam's angular jaw slowed in its chewing motion. Natalie paused when she saw the way his stare speared her.

"Why don't you just go ahead and ask it, Natalie?"

"Ask what?"

"Why don't you just ask whether or not my father was a true Irishman in another stereotypical sense? You want to know about his drinking habits."

Natalie carefully set down her ice water, acutely aware of penetrating dangerous territory without intent. Well, she was here now. Might as well deal with it.

"Eric told me that during the hearings, your mother testified that your dad was merely a social drinker. She insisted she never saw Derry drunk."

"And you don't believe her?" Liam asked with what struck Natalie as forced neutrality.

"I would believe it if *you* told me that was true."

He glanced up sharply. Their gazes held. Natalie realized muted live music was trickling in from the bar area of the restaurant—a piano, a drummer and a saxophone.

Liam was the first to break their stare.

"I try to give my mom the benefit of the doubt, even if Deidre never has. I think my mother *believed* what she said in court was true."

"Deidre doubts your mother's opinion on the matter?" Natalie asked, referring to Liam's eldest sister.

"Yeah," Liam said broodingly. "That's why Deidre never

comes back to Harbor Town, or at least that's what my brother, Marc, has insinuated. Deidre has never spoken to me about it, but I guess she holds my mom responsible for being in denial about my father's drinking."

Natalie sat back in the booth, stunned. "What do *you* think, Liam?"

He jabbed at a chunk of chicken but he didn't eat it.

"I remember him drinking regularly when he came home from work. It mellowed him, made him more cheerful. He seemed to need it to unwind. I never even thought about it, until after the crash. I never saw him drunk, but the truth is…"

He set down his fork abruptly and looked across the table at her. "One of my dad's closest friends at the end of a hard day was a bottle of whiskey."

"Thank you for telling me," she said quietly after a strained moment. He nodded and picked up his fork.

Natalie exhaled with difficulty. She could tell by the tension in his face it hadn't been an easy admission for him to make. It might have even been the first time he'd ever admitted it out loud.

And he'd done it in front of her—a Reyes. She resisted an urge to reach across the table and place her hand on top of his in gratitude.

In compassion.

"So…" she began shakily, determined to get them back on steady ground. "We can safely say that, although your father was no stranger to drinking, his behavior on the night of the crash was unusual. He was bitter and surly that night, when he was usually the essence of charm. He typically drank socially, or at home, but you never saw him heavily intoxicated. He likely drank alone at some point that night. Well past his normal limit."

"He *wanted* to get smashed," Liam stated bluntly.

"Yeah," Natalie whispered. "But *why?*"

Liam shook his head, obviously frustrated at not knowing the answer. "Most people get totaled like that when they're upset about something—breakups, sudden deaths...stuff like that."

"Right. Nothing like that happened in your family, though?"

"Nothing that I know of."

"Your mother and father...were they getting along okay? Did you ever hear any fighting?" she asked hesitantly.

"No. I was only fifteen at the time, I know, but I'd say the same thing now as an adult. My mom and dad seemed to have a great marriage. They were like kids together sometimes. My mom has never really gotten over my dad's death."

Neither of them spoke for a moment as Natalie tried to incorporate this information into what she already knew.

"The fact that he came to Harbor Town on a Tuesday— that's got to be relevant. He must have learned about something or found something out in Chicago and that was what upset him," Liam said, breaking the silence.

"Something about the Langford investigation, maybe?" Natalie wondered.

Liam shook his head. "No, like I said, he knew no charges were going to be pressed in regard to the SEC's investigation."

"Maybe he found out some other insider secret at his company, some wrongdoing that no one knew about. And it upset him."

Liam grimaced. "Maybe, but that doesn't seem to fit."

"Why?"

He paused, as if searching for the right words. "You had to know my dad. The way he acted on the night of the crash—it wasn't like a 'business' thing. It seemed...personal."

"You were really struck about what Roger Dayson said

about coming upon your dad that night on the beach, weren't you?" she asked quietly.

"I can't stop thinking about it," Liam admitted gruffly. "I can't even fathom it, to be honest. I can't picture it in my mind, my dad standing on that beach sobbing."

Neither of them spoke while Natalie finished her dinner. An oppressive fog seemed to have settled around them. One haunting thought kept echoing around in her mind.

She was the one responsible for putting Liam through this ordeal. What right did she have, to make him suffer for his father's mistake?

"To hell with this," Liam said so abruptly she started. He hitched his chin and grabbed her hand where it'd been resting on the table. "Let's go dance."

"Oh, I don't think—"

"What? You're not going to try and tell me you don't like dancing," he said, a small smile flickering across his mouth.

She couldn't tell him her like or dislike of dancing wasn't what was causing her to hesitate. It was the idea of being in Liam's arms.

She let him draw her out of the booth, but she shoved on her glasses first. The bar and dance floor might be crowded.

He didn't let go of her hand as they walked through the intimate dining room toward the bar. Natalie breathed a small sigh of relief when she saw there were only two other couples slow dancing to a jazz classic on the small dance floor. Liam turned and slid his left hand along her waist, his body instantly shifting to the beat of the music.

He pulled her closer, his hand spreading along the middle of her spine. Their bodies brushed together.

It was just a dance. Natalie knew this.

Her *mind* knew it; yet her body seemed to be screaming that it was something much, much more.

She stared blindly at a spot just below Liam's shoulder

while the band played. Her heart began to beat erratically when she felt him lower his head. His chin turned, nuzzling her, his short goatee whisking across her temple.

"It's like holding on to a dream, feeling the way you move."

She glanced up—couldn't have stopped herself if she'd tried. What he'd said didn't seem to match up to his expression. He looked strange...like he was irritated...or torn?

"Don't think I go around saying crap like that," he added stiffly. "I mean...it...it wasn't crap. It was the truth. Honestly." She saw his strong throat ripple as he swallowed.

An uncontrollable wave of sensation went through her at the sight of Liam Kavanaugh looking uncomfortable.

Liam Kavanaugh.

She ducked her head. Natalie couldn't decide what had stunned her more, the excitement caused by his warm breath and hoarse whisper in her ear or his unexpected revelation. His compliment had been undeniably sweet, but also electric somehow...erotically charged.

Why had that been?

Her heart fell to the vicinity of her belly when she realized why.

Because despite Liam's reputation as a charming playboy, she'd believed every word he'd said.

Her body buzzed with sensual awareness. As if Liam knew this perfectly, he pulled her closer. Her breasts pressed tight against his ribs. Their hips moved together. The music flowed not just through her, but Liam as well, joining them...entwining them. She couldn't decide where his heat began and hers ended.

She couldn't help but consider in wonder what it would be like to move even more intimately with Liam, to be joined with him so deeply that she felt his heartbeat at her very core.

The shivery sound of the drummer's brush lightly caressing the cymbals caused a tingling sensation to mount beneath her skin. The music ceased. She leaned her head back and peered up at Liam dazedly. His hand shifted as he drew off her glasses.

She peered up at him through eyelids that had gone heavy. His expression went hard. His nostrils flared. For some reason, his fearsome expression made her lips part in anticipation.

The saxophone wailed the opening notes to a new song. Natalie blinked. The two other couples were leaving the dance floor. Their faces were so bland, as if they hadn't noticed the magic of the moment at all.

The thought penetrated her sensual lassitude. She started out of Liam's arms. He didn't say anything when she took her glasses from him, donned them and walked toward the dining room.

They hardly spoke for the next several minutes, the one exception being when Liam grabbed the bill from her when they returned to the table.

"You shouldn't have to pay, it's a business exp—"

She pulled up short when she saw the expression on Liam's face. She'd been about to say the dinner was a business expense, but he'd halted her with a glance. He flipped a credit card into the leather folder. They waited in silence while the waiter returned, and the silence still hadn't broken once they got in the car and reached the outskirts of Harbor Town.

Natalie wasn't being silent to be obstinate. She was being quiet because her thoughts were coming too fast and chaotic to form a coherent sentence. Had she really been so keyed into him out there on the dance floor that she'd lost all sense of time, or purpose…or self? She'd known she was uncommonly attracted to Liam, but this was…unprecedented, in her experience.

And why was he so silent and somber? She wondered nervously as she gave him a sideways glance as he drove. His shirt showed up starkly white in the darkness, lit up as it was with moonglow. Despite all her uncertainty about the wisdom of her desire, she longed to ask him into her town house. But maybe—given his withdrawal—he wouldn't be interested? Surely he was second-guessing his occasional moments of attraction toward her, as well.

Second-guessing it…regretting it?

Liam had turned on the air-conditioning, but the atmosphere seemed to froth and boil in the small confines of the car. At last, he pulled into her driveway and the car came to a halt. He remained turned in profile, confusing her even more.

"Thank you for dinner," she tried to say, but her nervousness made her voice come out as a whisper. "Liam?" she asked when he didn't respond, just repositioned his hands on the top of the steering wheel.

"Yeah?"

"Are you…are you going to tell me about the meeting with your mother?" Natalie asked, suspecting the topic was partially responsible for his strange mood.

His face was cast with shadows, but she could feel his stare when he turned his head. "There isn't much to tell. I told her I was trying to gather information to better understand what Dad was going through when he caused the accident. I asked her about him coming home from the city on the night of the crash. She essentially told me I was being disrespectful to my father's memory and that I was a huge disappointment to her for agreeing to investigate the matter."

"Oh, no," Natalie whispered.

He laughed mirthlessly and reached for her hand. He pulled it into his lap.

"It's okay. She was just taken off guard. I breached her defenses unexpectedly, if you know what I mean, so she had to let go with the heavy artillery."

"Still…I'm sorry. It was never my intention to alienate you and your mother."

"I know that," Liam replied. Natalie became highly aware of the side of her hand resting on his muscular thigh and the way he stroked her wrist and thumb with warm, calloused fingertips. "Truth is, I'm mad at myself."

"Why?" Natalie asked.

"I should have asked her years ago. I've been a coward, colluding with her silence."

"No," Natalie protested warmly, leaning forward. "You're not a coward. That's ridiculous. It's like you said—families keep this stuff close. It's normal that you and your brother and sister have followed Brigit's lead in that regard."

His low grunt sounded doubtful, but Natalie knew she likely wasn't going to talk him out of his opinion.

"And so you told her that it was me who had asked you to do the investigation?"

"Yeah," he said. He seemed preoccupied as he watched himself stroke her hand. She, too, was distracted. It was hard to concentrate while Liam touched her.

"Your mother couldn't have been very thrilled about that."

He looked up. "No. She wasn't. That was about when she accused me of agreeing to investigate my father just because you were pretty. Apparently my mother thinks you charmed me into it, and I was too helpless to refuse."

Natalie gave an uncomfortable laugh. "I know that made you mad."

"It did." He turned her hand and laced his fingers through hers. Natalie responded naturally and closed her hand, holding him. Her heartbeat started to throb against her eardrums.

"But like I told you yesterday, she was partially right," Liam continued.

Natalie searched out his features in the dim light and saw the moonlight gleaming in his eyes.

"I do want you, Natalie," he admitted with disarming honesty. "I have since that night I saw you on the beach."

A swooping sensation occurred in her belly. She couldn't identify it as nervousness or excitement. He wanted her...as in wanted her in bed.

Liam Kavanaugh. Wanted *her*.

Awkward, self-conscious, inexperienced, scarred Natalie.

He gave a small, incredulous laugh. Natalie realized several taut seconds had elapsed while her brain had tried to compute Liam's words.

"You're not going to say anything, are you? About the fact that I just said I wanted to make love to you?"

"I'm not so sure it'd be...wise," she finally replied in a cracking voice.

"Yeah, I'd figured out that much myself, believe it or not. Knowing doesn't seem to be quieting the need any. Not a bit," he added wryly under his breath. For a few seconds, the silence stretched.

"But this has got nothing to do with wisdom," Liam said suddenly. He released her hand only to bury his hands in her hair. Natalie sat in the car seat, frozen as he furrowed his fingers through the long strands. She couldn't see his face, but she sensed his intensity.

"I've been wanting to do this all night. It ought to be made illegal for you to hide your hair. It's so soft."

Something swelled in her chest at the sound of awe in his deep voice.

Her hair slid through his fingers as he released it. His hands settled on her jaw, bracketing her face. The gesture struck her as tender...cherishing even. His head lowered over her and he spoke a fraction of an inch next to her lips.

"Tell me that you feel it, too."

She couldn't squeeze a word out of her throat, so she just nodded once.

And then he was kissing her, and everything faded away—her inexperience, their history, the tragedy, the hurt...the unanswered questions.

Nothing existed but Liam's hungry mouth and her own erupting need.

Chapter Seven

He felt her heat beneath him; he felt her soften. The whole-hearted consent of her body was even sweeter to him than her small nod of agreement had been.

Desire roared through his veins when she put her hands on his shoulders and caressed the muscles, making it the hardest trial of his life to keep a tight reign on himself. He couldn't stop his hands from moving, though. As he discovered the secrets of Natalie's mouth more thoroughly, his palms and fingers explored the mysteries of her body. She was like magic made into flesh: all taut, delicious curves and supple straight lines. He ran his hands from the indentation of her waist to her hips, finding the swell intoxicating. He settled on those curves and caressed them softly.

Her taste was like lust double-distilled.

When he realized he was quickly getting drunk on it, he sealed their kiss with effort. Her kisses were so sweet, but her occasional hesitance made him suspect she wasn't all that experienced. He should go slowly with her or he'd risk ruining things. He couldn't stop himself from plucking at her damp, warm lips, though. His hands moved, seemingly of their own accord, sweeping up the sides of her body.

He gave a restrained groan at the sensation of her full breasts against his palms. The rough sound seemed to startle her.

"It's okay," he murmured. He lifted his head and watched her exquisite face cast in moonlight as he pressed the center of her breasts into his palm. "I know I said I wanted to make love to you, but I'm not going to tonight. I just want to touch you a little. You're beautiful."

"I am not," she replied in a choked voice.

"You *are*. I'm going to show you some day just how beautiful you are. If you'll let me."

She blinked. Perhaps she'd been surprised at his intensity, but he'd stated a simple truth. He didn't know precisely when it had happened, but it had become an imperative for him to show Natalie Reyes how bright she shone in his eyes.

Her lips parted and he nuzzled them with his own, a bee drawn to honey.

"Does that feel good?" he murmured huskily as he cradled the weight of her breasts in his palms and whisked his thumbs over two taut peaks. It aroused him immensely, how responsive she was to his touch. He could feel the stiffness of her nipples directly through her bra.

"Yes."

He caught that small whisper with his brushing lips, treasuring it. He went very still when she began to move her hands, touching his upper arms lightly at first, then squeezing his biceps in her palms.

He lowered his head, the need to plunge back into the warm, wet cavern of her mouth too overwhelming at that moment to restrain himself. She jumped when something thumped against the passenger door.

Hard.

Liam reacted instinctively when he saw a hulking shadow outside the window. He unlocked his car door—leaving Natalie's locked—and got out of the car rapidly. If whoever was standing outside the passenger door was a threat, he'd be a sitting duck trapped in the car, unable to do anything to protect Natalie. He cursed himself for not carrying his weapon, but it was Harbor Town, for Christ's sake, and he wasn't even technically the chief of police yet.

"Get away from that door," he barked at the man who stood on the other side of the car. The figure was as tall as Liam, which was alarming. He experienced a mixed feeling of annoyance and relief when the man's features were revealed by moonlight.

"You get away from my sister and get the hell out of here, and I'll think about it, Kavanaugh," was Eric Reyes' harsh reply.

"Great," Liam muttered under his breath when he heard Natalie unlock her door. Liam and Eric had never gotten along. The last time he'd seen the great doctor was at the opening ceremony for the Family Center over a year ago, where they'd kept a wary distance from each other out of respect for the occasion and Mari Kavanaugh.

The last time he'd seen Reyes before that, the two of them had almost had a fistfight in the parking lot of Jake's Place.

"Eric! What are you doing here?" Natalie said when she opened the car door.

Eric unglued his glare on Liam and transferred his gaze to his sister. "I came to see you. Maybe you haven't noticed, but I do tend to do that, now and then. What are *you* doing?"

A tense silence ensued. Eric's voice had been thick with sarcasm and fury. Liam didn't have to see Natalie's face to sense how uncomfortable she must be feeling at that moment. Surely Eric had seen enough through the steamy windows to know precisely what they'd been doing.

"Don't use that sanctimonious tone of voice with her," Liam growled. "She wasn't doing anything wrong. You're the one who sneaked up on us and scared her half to death."

"Be quiet, Kavanaugh," Eric commanded, pointing across the hood of the car. "This is none of your damn business."

"Wrong," Liam said quietly through a clenched jaw. "This is none of *your* damn business.

"*Stop* it. Both of you."

Liam paused and looked at Natalie as she rose from the car. Her face looked pale and tense in the moonlight.

"I'll talk to you tomorrow, Liam." He could tell by her pointed expression that she was warning him to drop it.

"What? Why are you going to be talking to *him?*" Eric demanded, glancing from her to Liam with a look of confusion and alarm on his face.

"Liam and I are working on something together," Natalie said.

"Yeah. I could see that," Eric replied sarcastically.

"Liam," Natalie said sharply when Liam started around the car. He came to a halt, scattering gravel beneath his feet, glaring at Eric all the while.

"It'll be okay. I'll talk to you tomorrow." The small tremor in her voice quieted Liam's fury more than anything.

Liam nodded. He remained standing by the car as he watched Natalie and her brother walk toward her town house.

Eric slammed the door behind him.

"Jesus, Nat."

Natalie shut her eyes when she heard the three, pointed syllables. She didn't bother to turn around but merely walked into her living room and tossed her purse on the couch.

"Do you want me to make some coffee?" she asked calmly.

"No, I don't want any coffee," Eric stormed. She finally turned to look at him. Her brother was a very handsome man—tall, dark and intense. Three quarters of the female staff at Harbor Town Memorial, where he practiced as an orthopedic surgeon, would have sacrificed a great deal to have Eric drop in on them unexpectedly on a balmy Harbor Town summer night.

Natalie wished fervently he'd go grace one of *their* door-steps and leave his little sister alone…the same little sister he'd just caught making out with a Kavanaugh.

Her cheeks burned at the memory and she started toward the kitchen determinedly. "I'm going to make myself some coffee, then."

"Why the hell are you dressed like that?" Eric demanded as he followed her into the kitchen.

Natalie opened a cupboard and paused, feeling regretful. Eric had sounded positively flummoxed. Seeing her with Liam must have been like taking an unexpected blow to the head, though he'd have been confused and protective enough finding her steaming up the windows in a car with any man. Natalie didn't date that much, after all, and her brother had been the only witness to a few of her unsuccessful attempts during her early and mid-twenties. Eric had been the only witness to her hurt and tears when things had gone bad on those occasions.

He may be annoying at times, but he was her only family. Ever since their mother had died when she was eleven, he'd been both brother and father to her, taking on the full responsibility of an adult and caregiver at age eighteen.

If anyone deserved to scowl at her odd association with Liam Kavanaugh, it was Eric. Knowing that didn't particularly decrease her annoyance with his presence at the moment, though.

"What do you mean why am I dressed like that?" she asked, her irritation leaking into her voice, despite her former thoughts.

"Your hair, it's…" He paused and made a comical gesture around his head. "And that top you're wearing…" He couldn't seem to come up with the right word to describe it, but he persisted, unfortunately. "It's not really your style, is it?"

"You can't expect me to wear a business suit out on a date."

It took her a few seconds to register the ringing silence.

"You went on a date with *Liam Kavanaugh?*"

"Sort of," Natalie replied, already wishing she could take the words back. It was too late now. "Like I said, we're working on something together."

"What?"

Natalie exhaled and tossed the bag of coffee onto the counter. She started to tell him about her idea to hire Liam to investigate Derry Kavanaugh's state of mind on the night of the crash. By the time she'd finished, her brother had gone tight-jawed and pale behind his tan.

"Why didn't you tell me you planned on doing this?" he asked when she'd finally finished.

"I knew you'd worry about me if I did. I knew you'd tell me not to dwell on the past. But I'm not like you, Eric. I…I can't seem to let it go."

"There's nothing to be gained by this. Nothing," he said bleakly.

"You're wrong. I've already learned so much more about Derry Kavanaugh. He already seems more real to me, more human."

"He killed our mother and nearly killed you. You spent a good portion of time in a hospital, thanks to him. You endured constant pain, and countless surgeries and grueling rehabilitation. How much more *real* can the man be to you?" he asked.

"That was *my* reality," Natalie said shakily. "That was *ours*. I want to know what drove *him* to do what he did. I have to know."

"Why can't you let it rest?" Eric roared.

"Because *I'm* not resting," Natalie shot back. "If you've found peace by envisioning Derry Kavanaugh as the devil incarnate, then more power to you. I'm not trying to change your mind. Don't try to change mine."

Her brother just stood there, looking shocked by her heated outburst. Natalie felt bad for that—how well she knew that Eric wanted her to be happy—but she didn't feel bad enough to apologize for telling the truth.

She turned and switched on the coffeepot. "What *did* happen that night our lives changed forever? The question haunts me. Maybe it's an unhealthy obsession, but I'm not going to stop trying to get all the answers I can find," she said in a quieter voice.

Eric sighed heavily. "And is it absolutely necessary for you to go on this quest with Liam Kavanaugh?"

Natalie met her brother's stare slowly. She sensed the double meaning to his question.

"It's my business, Eric. The only thing I can tell you is that I'm trying to be reasonable. I'll do my best not to get hurt."

The hard tilt to Eric's mouth told her loud and clear he didn't find her promise very reassuring.

"I haven't even fully gotten used to Mari being with a Kavanaugh, and she's just a friend. How do you expect me to react to my only sister seeing one?"

She gave her brother a wry glance before she reached for some coffee mugs.

"Don't jump to any conclusions about what you saw in the car," Natalie stated more firmly than she felt. "I'd hardly compare Liam and me to Marc and Mari Kavanaugh. I'm just getting to know him."

"Right."

She threw him a quelling glance before she poured him a cup of coffee. "I told you I can take care of myself. Give it a rest, Eric."

"That'll be about as easy as you putting this crash-quest thing to rest."

"I didn't say it'd be easy," Natalie told him as she handed him his cup. She sighed in relief when he accepted it.

No sooner had Liam parked his bike in the Harbor County Library parking lot the next morning than he saw Natalie walking toward him. He paused, appreciating the sight. It felt good, seeing her so unexpectedly. He'd wanted to check up on her since last night, but he didn't want to seem as territorial and rude as her brother, so he'd refrained.

Barely.

She was dressed casually despite the fact that it was a weekday. She wore a pair of jean shorts that showed off her long legs and a tangerine T-shirt that enhanced her tan— not to mention the shape of her breasts. He was glad to see she wore her hair down. Most of it anyway. She'd pulled the front out of her delicate face, but the back hung around her shoulders.

He'd never seen such a sexy tumble of curls in his life. Most women would be flaunting that hair as a prime asset. Not Natalie, though. She never flaunted much of anything.

Natalie gave him a quizzical look as she approached. He blinked when he realized he was just sitting on his bike and staring at her like a drooling idiot.

He dismounted. Before she could say something that would stop him, he tangled his fingers in her hair and palmed her jaw. His mouth lowered. He'd meant it to be a casual kiss of greeting, but even more significantly, a reminder of last night. He wasn't going backward, despite Eric's irritating interference. He'd told her his intentions, and they hadn't changed.

That's what he'd *meant* the kiss to be. But when he felt her slight gasp of surprise tickle his mouth, when her lips softened against his and he registered her sweet taste, he lingered longer than he'd intended.

"Are you playing hooky, Natalie Reyes?" he asked her against her lips a moment later.

"What?"

She looked up at him. She looked gorgeous, lips parted, cheeks flushed, a dazed expression on her face.

He glanced down at her casual clothing teasingly. "It's Friday—isn't that an official CPA workday?"

"I'm not playing hooky," she said, her forehead crinkling. She stepped back, looking two parts bewildered and one part irritated at herself for participating so enthusiastically in his kiss. He hid a smile. "It's a holiday weekend coming up, and I'm just not that busy today. I thought I'd help you look up information on DuBois Enterprises and Alerveret."

"Great. I could use the help," Liam said, warmed by the fact that she'd come to join him. Suddenly the day seemed bright with endless possibilities. "I'll take you out to lunch afterward."

He grabbed her hand and kissed the back of it, smiling when he saw her mouth open in surprise at his brimming enthusiasm.

"Come on, detective," he urged, tugging on her hand.

Operation kiss and distract, Liam thought amusedly as he led her through the parking lot. He would sneak beneath her defenses when she least expected it, then distract her before she had a chance to protest.

Before Natalie knew it, she wouldn't be the least bit surprised that he planned on kissing her every opportunity he got.

* * *

A little over an hour and a half later, they walked down on Ontario Avenue, deep in discussion.

"It doesn't make any sense," Natalie said. "Neither your father or Langford, Inc., seemed to have any connection to DuBois Enterprises or Alerveret Corporation. Maybe it was just a red herring, your father's interest in that news program."

"It might have been," Liam said thoughtfully as they turned down Main Street.

"You don't really think so, though, do you?" Natalie asked, examining his profile. This morning there was a slight scruff of whiskers on his jaw. His hair was a windblown chaos of burnished waves. He looked a little intimidating—disreputable, even—so his occasional bouts of unselfconscious warmth toward her struck Natalie as all the more potent. One second she'd been admiring the image of him with his long legs straddling the sleek machine. Next he'd dismounted and kissed her.

She suspected her heart had just finally resumed its normal pace about five minutes ago, thanks to that kiss. She still hadn't decided how she was supposed to respond to this new, playful, yet strangely determined Liam.

"I don't know," Liam replied, drawing Natalie out of her thoughts. "Nothing else seemed to be penetrating his misery on that night."

"Liam, what are you doing?"

He glanced back at her, obviously caught off guard by her sharp question, his hand still outstretched to open the door of the Captain and Crew restaurant.

"I said I'd take you out to lunch," he reminded her.

"It's not really necessary," Natalie said quickly. She checked her watch. "I probably should go home and change and get into work, after taking the morning off."

Liam turned and faced her. She couldn't see his eyes behind his sunglasses, but she sensed him studying her.

"Why do you let them do it?" he asked softly.

"What do you mean?"

He gave a subtle sideways nod in the direction of two men who were walking toward the restaurant entrance. The men's conversation broke off and they observed Liam and Natalie with interest before they disappeared into the Captain and Crew.

"People. Strangers. You let their curiosity, or their rudeness, or whatever the hell the case may be, dictate your actions," Liam said.

For a few seconds, she just stared up at him. He'd said it so evenly that it took a moment for his meaning—and her embarrassment—to soak into her consciousness. Her cheeks flamed.

"You don't know what you're talking about," she whispered.

"I think I do. You avoid crowded places. You don't like to have people look at you, so you steer clear of places like Jake's or the Captain and Crew. I wish you wouldn't let it get to you, Natalie."

"You have no right to judge me," she bit out. "You're the *last* person on earth who has the right to judge me."

She spun around, intent on departure. She gasped when Liam reached out, quick as a snake at the strike, and grasped her hand, halting her.

"I'm sorry," he said rapidly when she opened her mouth to tell him off. She paused when she saw the look of genuine regret on his face. "I really am. You're right. It has to be something you're comfortable with—not something I wish for."

Tears burned her eyelids. *Something I wish for.* She was

so confused, she couldn't manage to get out the question scalding the back of her tongue.

Why should he care one way or another how I feel in a public place?

He stepped closer. Her emotional turmoil only mounted when he cradled her jaw, his fingers caressing her cheek softly. She hadn't known him that long, but already she'd grown accustomed to this particular tender, prizing gesture. He used his other hand to remove her glasses and then he leaned in, pressing his forehead against hers.

"I just wish you could see yourself like I see you. You're beautiful, and not despite this." Her lungs ached in her chest, but she still couldn't draw breath as he gently traced her scar. He pressed a kiss at the corner of her eyelid, like a period at the end of a poignant sentence. "Because of it, Natalie. In part, at least. It's one of the many things that make you unique…and yes, beautiful."

A depthless font of uncertainty welled up in her chest at that moment. Several teardrops spilled from her eyes, spattering on Liam's skin.

"Let me go," she said, her throat too tight for anything but a whispered plea.

His fingers loosened reluctantly around her glasses when she tugged on them. Slipping them on, she turned and hurried down the street.

Natalie wasn't necessarily surprised when she saw Liam standing at her door later that evening, but she was extremely glad. She knew she'd behaved like a child earlier. She'd been regretting her insecurities so much that it'd been hard for her to concentrate at work, and she'd left early.

"Hi," she greeted Liam as she opened the screen door.

"I came to beg forgiveness, but I realize it might be a challenge for you," he told her wryly, his mouth quirked in a small half grin. "Do you think if I gave you a license to call me a tactless idiot as many times as you wanted all evening and made you dinner to boot, you could eventually get there?"

"You don't have to make me dinner." She studied her welcome mat like it held the mysteries of the universe. She shifted on her bare feet. "I'm the one who should say I was sorry. I overreacted."

A heavy silence followed her apology. Surely it would be a mistake to allow herself to spend time with him…to allow herself to fall for him. She couldn't begin to count the number of reasons why it would never work, the least of which was his vast experience with dating compared to her novice status. She would just end up making a fool of herself and getting hurt. Then, there was the fact that his association with her was causing major waves with his mother. He'd probably end up resenting her for creating so much drama in his personal life—

Liam gently pushed a stray curl off her forehead, interrupting her flow of catastrophic thinking. Since he stood a step below her on the stoop, her eyes were level with his mouth. His thumb skimmed over her cheek, and then across her lower lip.

"So what about dinner at my place? It'd be a great evening for a swim, too," he murmured distractedly, his gaze following the trail of his fingertip.

Natalie just stared for a few seconds, temporarily overwhelmed by his sudden nearness and stroking finger. He must have misunderstood the reason for her hesitation, because he added quickly, "I had a conversation with Jack Andreason earlier."

"The bartender?" Natalie asked breathlessly.

"Yeah. I'll tell you about it. Is it okay if I step into the AC while you get your suit? It's sweltering out here."

"Oh, of course. Please, come in," Natalie said quickly,

mortified to realize she'd left him standing outside the entire time.

"If you have a pair of swim shoes or rubber flip-flops or something, bring those, too," Liam called as she started down the hallway a moment later. "I haven't gotten around to having any sand poured at the beach, and it's rocky."

It wasn't until she'd hurriedly packed a canvas beach bag that Natalie realized how easily he'd smooth-talked her into accompanying him.

She was already regretting the decision by the time she followed Liam out to the driveway, her feet faltering when she saw his motorcycle. She recalled how she'd said she was disappointed because he hadn't driven it last night and mentally damned her bravado.

"Is this the first time you've been on a bike?" Liam asked her as he stored her bag and handed her a helmet. Natalie suspected from his overly casual tone he'd noticed her apprehension.

He mounted the bike, all sinuous long limbs and effortless male grace. The motorcycle roared to life. "No worries. You'll be safe with me." His flashing grin faded as he examined her. "I promise, Natalie."

Natalie seriously doubted about her safety when it came to Liam Kavanaugh, but she took the plunge anyway and got on the leather seat behind him, feeling every bit as awkward and foolish as Liam appeared comfortable and confident.

He turned his head so that she could see his profile.

"The only thing you've got to do is hold on. Tighter," he added when she looped her arms around his waist in an uncertain gesture.

He exited her driveway at a tame pace, but when he turned down Travertine Road, the bike took off like a rocket. Natalie felt her heart plummet to the vicinity of her navel, and she hung on to Liam for dear life.

Chapter Eight

It took a few seconds for the full experience of being on the motorcycle to penetrate her consciousness. When she pried open her eyes after a moment, she saw the houses and trees along Travertine zooming by in a colorful, blurred landscape. The machine felt alive beneath her, as if they were riding some wild animal while it gave off a mixture of a growl and a vibrating purr.

By the time they passed the old, handcrafted mailbox at the cottage, Natalie had abandoned herself to the experience. Her upper body pressed flush against Liam's back. Her cheek rested between his shoulder blades. She inhaled his scent— a subtle, fresh, spicy smell mixing with the clean fragrance of his laundered shirt. His body felt hard and supple in her encircling arms.

She was genuinely disappointed when Liam planted his feet on the gravel drive and the steel beast went silent.

Natalie clambered off the seat, removed the helmet and

idly began to smooth back her hair. She noticed Liam's quiz-zical look.

"What?" she asked as she readjusted a pin. "Why are you smiling like that?"

"You're the one who's smiling, Natalie." She paused when she heard the gruff intimacy of his voice. It struck her in a flash he was right. She'd been grinning like an idiot. What's more, her cheeks were hot. She brushed her fingertips across them in wonder.

She'd completely lost herself in the experience.

Feeling a little bewildered by her reaction, she busied her-self with claiming her canvas bag.

"You liked it," Liam said as he dismounted. He whipped off his glasses. "You liked it a lot."

Natalie gave him a severe glance for the smug satisfac-tion in his voice. When she saw the sparkle in his blue eyes, though, she couldn't help but join him in laughter.

Both of them were hot and sticky after the ride, so they agreed to swim first. Natalie exited the downstairs bathroom feeling self-conscious, wearing nothing but her bathing suit and a pair of flip-flops. Why hadn't she thought to bring a cover-up or towel?

She breathed a sigh of relief when she entered the empty kitchen and saw a large blue beach towel placed conspicu-ously on the kitchen table. Liam had obviously left it there for her. When she walked onto the terrace she saw him already down at the beach, the waves breaking around his calves. He turned and looked back at the sound of the screen door closing. He waved before he walked a few more feet into the water and pushed off the shore, shooting into the lake like a human projectile.

Her eyes remained fixed on him as she walked along the stone path between swaying prairie grass, cattails and sun-flowers. His muscular, tanned back flexed and shone next to the shimmering water. She placed her towel on a rock and carefully set her glasses upon it.

If this had been the first time she'd been with Liam, she would have jumped to the conclusion that he'd gone ahead of her because he was hot and craved a refreshing swim.

Now she knew different.

He'd given her space deliberately. He'd known she'd be self-conscious if he stood over her while she removed her glasses and dropped her towel. She'd underestimated him by assuming he was too self-confident to understand another person's insecurities.

She had a strong suspicion she'd underestimated Liam in a number of ways.

It embarrassed her that he'd seen her vulnerability. Her gratitude toward him was stronger, though. At least Natalie *thought* it was gratitude. She didn't know what else to call the ache in her chest she felt when she recognized his subtle acknowledgment of her feelings.

She waded in cautiously. She was hot from the summer sun and humidity, but as usual, Lake Michigan was frigid at first contact.

Liam turned a few feet away from the craggy breakwater and headed back toward shore. It was clear he came from a family of swimmers. He sliced through the water with an even, powerful stroke, making it look as easy as a hot knife carving through butter. In reality, Natalie knew from experience that swimming in the choppy water took a special skill, one she'd never fully mastered.

He surfaced a few feet away from her and knelt in the water.

"Still cold for August, huh?"

Natalie nodded, keeping Liam in the periphery of her vision as she stared at the gray water. If she stared too intently into the brilliant sunshine, her weak eyelid would involuntarily close. She didn't want Liam to notice that.

"You're such a good swimmer," she murmured.

"Thanks."

He stood abruptly, causing the water to splash loudly around him. He stepped closer to her, casting Natalie in his tall shadow. She exhaled in relief and glanced up at him. She realized he'd blocked the sun on purpose—to protect her. For a second or two, she waited for the dread and embarrassment to come, the feelings that usually resulted after being exposed.

They never did.

His gaze was so uncommonly soft; his blue eyes were so warm. She recalled what he'd said this afternoon in front of the Captain and Crew about her scar: *It's one of the many things that make you unique...and yes, beautiful.*

She returned his smile.

"I remember watching you swim at the beach when I was a girl," she said.

"Yeah?" he asked gruffly. He stepped closer and removed a strand of loose hair from her cheek with cool, damp fingertips.

She nodded as he tried to tuck the errant strand behind her ear. Her face was less than a foot away from his chest. His nipples were a dark copper color. They were erect from the cold water.

"I remember one summer you wore a pair of trunks that were the same color as the ones you're wearing right now—turquoise blue," she said in a rush. She felt his hand still in her hair. She kept her gaze fixed on his wet, muscular chest.

She was finally granted the ability to inhale when he resumed smoothing her hair. He stepped back, although he was careful to keep her cast in his shadow.

"I wish I could remember you," he said.

"No you don't. I mean...I'm glad you don't," she said with a laugh. "My mother usually wanted my hair short during the summers, because it was easier. It grows so fast, and it took her so long to brush out the snarls after a day at the beach. She just didn't have the time. She worked too hard. When I was ten or eleven, I looked like an adolescent boy—skinny arms and legs. It was one of the reasons I liked the beach—at least in my bikini, people knew I was a girl."

He chuckled. "I'll bet you were adorable. I can't picture you with short hair, though." His eyes flickered down over her shoulders and chest. "I definitely can't imagine you being mistaken for a boy."

Her cheeks heated from a mixture of pleasure and embarrassment.

"Were you shy? As a little girl?" Liam asked, his voice a low rumble.

"Yes," she said quietly as she watched her hands dance in the rippling water. "My mother used to say I was coming out of my shell, though. I'd become really involved in ballet classes and started doing recitals. Performing took me out of myself a little bit."

"You'd been at a ballet recital on the night of the accident."

She glanced up sharply. She'd been surprised by his statement, but Liam looked even more stunned at his own words.

"Sorry," he muttered. He glanced toward the beach, a strange expression on his face. "I have no idea where that came from. It just hit me all of a sudden. I must have read it in a newspaper, or heard it on the news back when I was a kid. When you mentioned the recitals, it just sort of sprung up out of nowhere from my memory."

Her surprise at his abrupt statement about the crash vanished in the face of his obvious discomfort.

"There's no need to apologize," she said, her voice even. "It probably was in the papers. My mother and I had been at a recital over in South Haven. We were driving home that night."

"You and your mother were close, weren't you?" he asked after a moment.

"Yes. Very close."

His gaze remained fixed on the beach. She saw his muscular throat convulse and she stepped toward him.

"It's okay to ask about her, Liam."

He glanced down at her sharply.

"I'm curious about you and your father, as well." She hesitated before she plunged ahead. Glimpsing his uncertainty had given her courage, for some reason. "I would have been curious even if it wasn't for the crash. I would have been, because of you."

For a few taut seconds, she couldn't read his expression. Then he muttered something under his breath she couldn't quite catch and his arms closed around her. She shivered at the contact of his cool, wet skin against hers. He must have felt it, because he pushed her tighter against him, surrounding her with his body, until his heat penetrated into her. He bent his neck and pressed the side of his head against hers.

Natalie suppressed a whimper of rising emotion as her arms wrapped around his waist. Being so suddenly enfolded in his embrace like that had affected her in a way she hadn't expected. It was a hug of compassion, an acknowledgment of their shared suffering.

As the seconds passed, however, and she became hyper-aware of Liam's near-naked body pressed intimately against her own, Natalie admitted the embrace meant more than compassion. Much more. Desire twined with all those other emotional threads: brilliant, golden and undeniable. His chin moved. He spoke in a low, gruff voice, his warm breath in her ear causing ripples of pleasure to course down her spine.

"This is a hell of a thing, isn't it?"

"Yes." No sound came out of her throat, but the right side of her mouth was pressed against the dense muscles of his chest. She knew he'd sensed her answer, just as she somehow knew he'd been referring to their strange association with one another, their past…the attraction between them that seemed to building to some kind of crescendo.

He trailed his large hand down her spine, and she shivered.

"Are you cold?" he murmured, his palm coming to rest just above her buttocks.

"Not…not really," she replied with breathless honesty.

He stepped back. The setting sun shone so brightly around his outline it was like he was a haloed hero from a dream in her dazzled eyes. It fit somehow, that description. Distantly, she realized her cheeks were wet with tears, but…she experienced no embarrassment under Liam's stare.

She felt strangely light-headed at the realization, liberated, her soul seemingly swelling upward, like a weight had just been lifted off her that she'd never known existed until now.

"Are you going to swim?" he asked her soberly.

She shook her head. She'd already plunged way deeper into these emotional waters than she'd ever intended.

"Let's go inside then," he said.

He took her hand and led her toward the beach.

He was happy that Natalie joined him on the terrace when he went out to grill their supper. Something had happened out there as they stood in the frigid waters of Lake Michigan. Some kind of barrier had melted away. The change in Natalie's manner toward him was subtle, but at the same time…

Miraculous.

Liam felt as if he had somehow gained the privilege of watching a flower bloom before his very eyes. Slowly, maybe…and tentatively, as if she was testing out the environment. But there could be no doubt of it.

Natalie trusted him enough to open up her inner world.

It humbled him a little, that realization.

He closed the lid of the smoking grill and listened as Natalie described the volunteer work she did for the Family Center—the treatment and family support facility for survivors of substance abuse that Mari Kavanaugh had opened last year. Apparently, Natalie volunteered a good chunk of her time in order to do the Center's books, plus she took on the responsibility of making sure the Center's licenses and operating guidelines were up to date and within required code.

"You make me feel like a shirker for just hammering a nail now and then," Liam said.

"You had that beautiful sign made. *Choose hope*," she said softly, repeating the quote Liam had requested for the sign he'd commissioned for the Family Center last year.

He couldn't have stopped himself for anything. He leaned down and pressed his mouth to her wistful smile. His heart felt like it skipped a beat when he felt her smile widen beneath his lips before she kissed him back; it drummed into double-time when she laced her fingers through his hair.

A sudden blast of smoke in his face was the only thing that stopped him from tossing down the spatula and sacrificing the salmon to the flames.

He'd rather have Natalie for dinner.

"So I guess we'll both be going to the Labor Day fundraiser Mari and Colleen have been planning this Sunday. Why don't we go together?" Liam asked after he'd coughed the smoke out of his lungs and hurriedly removed the salmon fillets from the grill before they turned to carbon. He turned off the gas and picked up the plate of steaming fish.

It took him a moment to realize she hadn't responded

immediately. He glanced at her. She wore a strange expression on her face—hesitant, pleased…wary?

"Okay, that'd be nice," she said, and the flicker of anxiety he'd felt for a second upon seeing her uncertainty vanished. He grinned in satisfaction. There could be no doubt about it this time.

He'd just officially asked Natalie Reyes out and she'd said yes.

The terrace was cast in the pinkish-gold hues of sunset as they ate. After supper, they pushed back their plates and talked almost nonstop until the crimson orb of the sun sank slowly into the dark blue waters of the lake.

"It's not as bad as it sounds," he said quickly at one point when he glanced up and noticed how set and pale Natalie's face had become as he described having his cover blown last year when he'd been investigating some corrupt cops. "I knew Tresedi wouldn't kill me without the consent of Maguire—Maguire ruled the pack—and the chances were pretty good my partner would find me before Maguire ever gave the order."

"The chances were *pretty good*," Natalie repeated, her voice flat with incredulity and anxiety.

"Mike Estes has never failed me before, and he didn't in this case," Liam repeated, referring to his former partner.

Natalie picked up her iced tea and took a large swallow. "It's so scary," she murmured. "You could have easily been killed at a dozen different times during that investigation. I don't understand how you did it, living so secretively…so dangerously for almost a year."

"It wasn't that bad. For the most part, I was just carrying on with my normal job."

"You make it sound like your 'normal' job was as safe as selling Tupperware. I, for one, am glad you decided to quit the Chicago P.D. and come to Harbor Town."

"Even a sinner deserves a couple of peaceful years, huh?" he teased.

"I have a feeling life would never be calm around you."

He leaned forward, his elbows on the table, as if her low voice had tugged at him like a magnet. Dusk had settled, soft and hushed. He stared at the feminine curve of Natalie's cheek as wisps of her hair fluttered against it.

"Take off your glasses." When he realized how blunt he'd sounded, he added softly, "Please."

She removed her glasses and set them on the table. Her face was beautiful in that pregnant moment when the day meets the night, enigmatic…sublime.

"Spend the night here."

Her expression stiffened. *"What?"*

"I don't want to take you home. I will, if you want me to, of course." When she didn't speak, he continued as if he thought he was making up for a dire mistake. "We don't have to…you know. Not if you're not ready. You can have the guest room."

"Liam…you say the strangest things sometimes," she said, disbelieving.

"You think it's strange that I don't want you to go home?"

For a few seconds she just stared at him, her mouth open. "No," she whispered. She turned her chin. "No, I don't think that part is strange."

"Which part, then?"

The glow from the lights in his kitchen allowed him to see her elegant throat convulse as she swallowed. He hated the separation of the table between them.

At that moment, he despised all the barriers between him and Natalie.

"You never told me what Jack Andreason told you," she said so quietly he almost didn't hear her.

"You never answered me about staying here with me tonight," he countered in a voice just as hushed.

"I haven't made up my mind yet. Now tell me about Jack."

Liam sighed and leaned back in temporary defeat. He could tell by the hint of steel in her soft voice he shouldn't push the topic for now. He forced his mind to focus on the conversation he'd had with Jack Andreason that afternoon.

"I drove over to St. Joseph—that's where Jack lives now. He bought a little restaurant on the beach. Jack was tending bar when I got there. He actually recognized me right away."

"He did? Did you know him well when you were young?"

Liam shook his head distractedly as he played with his napkin. "Nah. He said he recognized me because I looked like Dad."

"Oh." After a pause, she asked hesitantly, "Do you? Look like Derry, I mean?"

A vivid memory came to him: his father holding out a color photo. The boy in the picture might have been Liam himself, standing on a Harbor Town beach when he was twelve years old, so lean he was almost more bone than flesh, his skin darkened to a golden brown, a cocky little half-smile ghosting his lips.

Of course it hadn't been Liam, but his father at the same age.

He remembered glancing up from the photo to see the knowing sparkle in his father's eye; he recalled the rush of pleasure that filled him in that moment...the intangible bond he'd felt with the man who stood before him.

"I look a little like him, yeah," Liam muttered.

"And you asked Jack about what you saw on the tape?"

Liam nodded. "He said he'd never seen my dad the way that he was on that night."

"And he knew Derry fairly well, right?"

"My father had belonged to the Silver Dunes Country Club for seven years. He and Jack were friendly."

"Did he give any theories about why he thought your father was so upset?"

Liam gave her a wry glance. "He said something similar to what Roger Dayson said the other night. Apparently Dad's bad mood had the same effect as a cornered dog baring its teeth. Jack remembered the way my father barked at him to leave the television alone when he started to change the channel."

"Did he have the impression that it was just that segment your father was interested in?" Natalie asked.

"He couldn't recall for sure. The next thing he knew, he saw my father getting up to go. He did say one thing that struck me."

"What?"

"He said that for a second there, he thought my father looked mad enough to vault over the bar, but he couldn't decide if my dad wanted to hit him or the television screen. According to Jack, he looked a little wild."

"That's so strange. What do you think, Liam?" she asked, leaning forward intently with her elbows on the table. She wasn't asking idly. It seemed clear from Liam's somber expression he'd done some wrestling with his thoughts on the matter.

He paused before replying. "That news story was about the corporate takeover, so we researched the companies. But Jack couldn't see that television screen like I could on that surveillance video—or like my father could. Lincoln DuBois himself was being interviewed for the segment."

"You think your father could have been upset about Lincoln DuBois? But I thought you said your parents didn't know him."

"He's a celebrity in the financial world, but my parents

never mentioned knowing him personally. Is Lincoln DuBois even alive? I never hear about him on the news anymore. He used to be a media favorite, didn't he? He's got to be alive—he didn't look all that old in that television segment."

"He's alive."

Liam's head shot up with interest. "He is? How do you know?"

Natalie nodded. "I read about it in an old *Forbes* article while you were combing through the newspaper references this morning. DuBois has had several strokes in the last two years, and I guess they caused some serious functional impairments. According to the article, he's still running the company, but he does so from his Lake Tahoe home. He lives an isolated life."

Liam's brows shot up with interest.

"What part of Tahoe?"

"South Lake. Apparently, that's where he grew up. DuBois comes from money, in addition to creating an empire on his own. His father was a multimillionaire—made his fortune in real estate and cattle. DuBois always kept it as his home base, even though his major corporate hubs are in both San Francisco and New York."

"You're brilliant," Liam mumbled, preoccupied.

"I just read an article. Liam…what's wrong?" she asked, leaning forward.

He blinked and pushed his chair back. "Nothing. The mosquitoes are starting to bite. Come on, let's go inside."

Her mind started jumping around as if she'd just consumed two turbocharged lattes as she followed Liam inside the screen door. Their conversation about Derry had distracted her for a few minutes, but now she couldn't stop thinking about Liam asking her to spend the night.

The fact that she was thinking about accepting his proposal

shocked her even more. If she agreed to sleep with Liam, she'd have to tell him she'd never had sex.

She grasped wildly for a safe topic of conversation as she helped Liam do the dishes, but her rising anxiety got the best of her. Luckily, Liam didn't appear to be uncomfortable at all in a silence that felt suffocating to Natalie. He was absorbed in his thoughts, but he seemed to rise out of them as he shut the dishwasher.

"Do you want to see what I've done to the cottage so far? I'd like your opinion on a couple of things."

"Of course," she murmured.

"I don't want to waste money loading it up with furniture when I'm not really sure what I want yet," Liam explained as he led her through the sparsely furnished living room.

"That's a good idea. This place has such a light, open feel to it, like it was meant to be filled with clean lake air and sunlight. It wouldn't do to cram it full with a bunch of heavy furniture. I pictured a golden tan for the walls in this room, and then filling it with rich browns and ivories. It'd make it look like a sunlit globe in the mornings. When I thought about buying the cottage, the first thing I fantasized about doing was restoring the fireplace to its former glory," Natalie said as she ran her hand across the age-and-smoke-dulled wood. The magic she'd once felt sneaking into the rundown, yet still elegant old home, returned to her full force. "It's made of carved African mahogany and Carrera white marble."

Liam looked impressed. "My mom told me I was nuts when I said I was considering slapping some paint on the mantle. She could tell it was fine craftsmanship, but she didn't know all those details. How'd you find out that stuff?"

"I dug up a few historical facts on the cottage when I was thinking about buying it. George Myerson, the original owner, was the president of the Pacific Railway and he commissioned Ellison Raft of Chicago to design the place. I copied the old articles I found. I still have them somewhere, if you'd like me to give them to you."

"That'd be great, thanks," Liam said as he led her up the stairs. Natalie followed him into the large, west-facing room.

"I can't figure out what I should do with this space," he said.

"Myerson used it as a saloon—a kind of nineteenth century Guys Only Club, where he and the other men played pool, smoked cigars, told fishing stories…avoided their wives," Natalie added with a small smile. She opened a door, which led to what looked like an enormous closet or small room, and stepped over the threshold. "This was the actual bar in here, where he stored spirits and wine."

"Huh," Liam spoke from just behind her. "I've found the local expert on my house. How lucky am I?"

Natalie laughed and turned to face him. Her smile faded when she realized how close he was. He'd been peering into the small room from behind her, his arm braced above her head on the door frame. His tall, rangy body blocked her exit.

She couldn't decide if her hammering heart was trying to tell her to escape or submit to her urge to stay put.

"I'm not an expert in the slightest. You could find all this stuff out by doing a little research."

He ducked his head so that his warm breath brushed against her nose and cheek. "That sounds much less exciting than hearing all this wisdom straight from Natalie Reyes' mouth. Especially," he continued, his low, vibrating voice causing a shiver to skitter down her spine, "when it's such a lovely mouth."

"Liam."

She'd meant to say his name in a warning tone, but instead, it'd sounded like an uncertain plea of longing. Liam brushed his mouth against hers in a coaxing kiss, his lips warm and firm.

"Don't be afraid of me, Natalie."

Her lips moved, and Natalie herself couldn't be sure if they did so to speak, or to caress Liam's coaxing mouth. "I'm not afraid of you."

His hand remained braced on the doorframe, but he placed his other hand on her lower back and then palmed her hip. His lips shaped hers gently and Natalie felt those careful, deliberate movements all the way in the core of her body.

"You're...afraid...of something," Liam muttered, taking small bites of her lips. His hand moved, stroking her back. Natalie's spine arched slightly against the pressure, as if her flesh were melting against the heat of his palm. Liam took a step closer and lowered his other arm. His hands bracketed her waist as he continued to kiss her, his mouth still closed, but his movements grew increasingly feverish.

"What, Natalie? What are you afraid of?" He lifted his head, pinning her with a blazing stare. He pulled her closer, their bodies melding into that supreme fit that she recalled all too perfectly.

"This," she admitted softly.

He just stared down at her for a moment, his features cast in part-shadow. She had little doubt that Liam knew she referred to the heat that resonated between their pressing bodies at that very moment, the electric charge that always seemed to occur whenever they touched.

"It's probably a bad idea, Liam," she whispered, even as her forearms slid against his waist and her fingertips discovered the muscles of his back through the fabric of his shirt.

"It might be unwise," he granted gruffly. His head lowered. "But it feels unstoppable."

He leaned down, forcing her back to arch against the firm hold of his hands at her waist. All the restraint he showed in his former, questing kisses evaporated. She was submerged in Liam's heat, his possessive kiss…his fierce spirit.

And she knew he was right. They'd unleashed a force of nature neither one of them could control.

Chapter Nine

Natalie altered beneath the power of Liam's kiss, transformed into a sensual creature, suddenly unafraid of the deep passions that frothed at her core. It was a little like losing herself in the dance. When she allowed the movement to overcome her, she forgot the audience or any expectations it might have of her.

She craned upward, wild for more of his taste, desperate to quench her tingling nerve endings with the hard pressure of his body. She slid her tongue next to his and treasured the sound of his low moan of arousal. He stroked her hips and back with increasing excitement, molding her flesh against his, as though he knew he was creating a fire beneath her skin with the added friction. Natalie began to explore him as well. Her opened hands found the upward slant from his ribs to his chest fascinating. It was like holding the essence of power in her very hands, caressing Liam.

That feeling of power spread to her when she sensed how much he liked her touch.

He groaned into her mouth. Their tongues dueled sensually and she felt him grow even harder, his muscles flexing beneath her seeking fingertips, his arousal flagrantly obvious next to her straining body.

He sealed their kiss, but, as if he couldn't get enough of her mouth, he continued to nip at her lips. Natalie responded in kind, nibbling at him feverishly. He tasted so good, it wasn't enough. Her tongue slicked along his lower lip as if it had a mind of its own.

He groaned roughly. The next thing Natalie knew, he'd shifted her in his arms and she was airborne. Her mind and body both seemed to be flying, falling headlong into the pool of sensual pleasure Liam always created with his touch. The bedroom where he brought her was dim—only the light from the hallway illuminated it. He laid her on the bed with what struck Natalie as exquisite care, as though he thought she'd break.

She stared up at him, her breath coming fast and ragged. Anxiety had started to rise again, but the image of Liam looking down at her held her so spellbound that she couldn't focus on her nervousness overly much. His expression was rigid with arousal. She could just make out the gleam in his eyes as he watched her. He brushed back the hair on her brow in a gentle gesture. His hands felt hot and dry next to her skin. He looked down at her as he rubbed the tip of his thumb over her lower lip. As if he'd pushed a secret button, Natalie parted her mouth to better feel his touch.

His nostrils flared with arousal.

"You're so beautiful," he murmured. "I want to see all of you. Can I undress you?"

Natalie nodded, unable to speak. She didn't necessarily

believe in the truth of his words on a personal basis, but in that moment, she could read his expression perfectly.

Liam thought she was beautiful.

His stare remained melded to hers as he reached for the hem of her shirt and lifted it over her head. When the neckline snagged on her bun, he gently loosened it and then tossed aside her shirt. She felt his fingers moving in her hair.

"How many of these things do you have to use to keep all that hair on your head?" she heard him murmur in amusement as he drew out one pin after another. He kept one hand on her body, stroking her shoulder and neck, as if he didn't want to lose physical contact with her even as he undressed her. Natalie suspected he'd sensed her nervousness, and was reassuring her with his humor and touch.

She smiled. "I don't know. I don't count."

"Twelve," Liam said a moment later as he deposited the last bobby pin on the table.

"Thank you for solving that little mystery for me," she said shakily. The flicker of amusement she experienced faded when she saw his face as he ran his fingers through her unbound hair.

He tried to smile at her comment, but he looked strained as he gazed down at her wearing nothing but a bra and low-riding shorts, her hair spread across the pillow. He extended one long finger and traced the curve of her hip to her waist. She shivered when he touched the side of her ribs. Her nipples prickled with pleasure. She'd had no idea she had so many sensitive spots on her body until Liam showed them to her.

"You were made by a true artist, Natalie Reyes."

"So were you," she whispered.

"You got some extra attention." The muscles of his face were so tense with desire that he looked almost grim in the dim light as he reached behind her to unfasten her bra. As he slid it from her body, the combination of the cool air and

Liam's heated stare made her bare breasts tingle. She didn't shrink from his gaze. Why would she, when he looked at her as he did at that moment?

"You're so pretty."

The hint of awe in his tone made her reach for him. She brought him down to her, wincing in pleasure when he placed his mouth at the upper curve of her left breast. His moving, caressing lips seemed to create a trail of fire as he explored her contours.

"So soft," he murmured.

His palm came up to cradle her right breast, as if testing the weight of it. She knew how strong Liam was; she sensed his power like a tightly coiled spring. The gentleness of his touch contrasting with all that strength made her heart seem to swell in her rib cage. His hands were large, and his fingertips blunt, but they became precise instruments for evoking pleasure when touching her.

She shivered when he gently scraped his teeth over a rib just below her breast. Her nipples puckered tight at the sensation. As if Liam had known precisely the effect his caress would have, he slipped the sensitized crest of her breast between his lips.

Natalie's breath caught at the feeling of being enclosed in his warm mouth. He applied a soft suction and laved his tongue over the beading nipple and Natalie forgot how to breathe, the pleasure that coursed through her was so sharp... so imperative.

She whimpered with need. As if desire connected them, Liam growled deep in his throat at the same moment, the sound vibrating into her breast and down to her heart.

She called his name in a plaintive plea, and he lifted his head reluctantly.

"You taste so good," he muttered, sounding a little incredulous. Natalie moaned when he pressed his entire face to her abdomen and nuzzled her belly button with his nose. His whiskers scraping gently against the skin should have sent her into a fit of ticklish laughter, but instead, his actions created a hot, thick sensation in her lower belly. The sensation only increased when he opened his mouth and she felt the heat of his mouth penetrating her.

He rose over her and took her mouth heatedly. It was a wild kiss, a torrid one. It told Natalie loud and clear how much he wanted her.

She treasured that knowledge.

The tips of her breasts ached. She pressed closer to his chest, desperate to alleviate the prickling sensation. He groaned into her mouth and reached between them, his fingers finding the fastenings of her shorts. Then his fingers were touching her—gentle and knowing.

Natalie stared blindly at the ceiling fan, poised on a precipice of bliss, listening to Liam whisper an anthem of desire to her, overwhelmed by sensation. She clung to his shoulders as if she thought they were the only things saving her from falling. "You're even sweeter than I thought you'd be…and I imagined plenty."

It suddenly struck her through a thick haze of arousal what was happening. She was supposed to let go…surrender to this hot, building need. Surrender to Liam.

The realization felt huge in that moment…frightening. If she gave herself in this physical way, she doubted she could ever go back. Her soul, too, would be his. And Liam didn't know this about her; that she was a novice when it came to love. For him, this was just the inevitable conclusion of two people desiring each other. He could give of himself in just a physical sense, while Natalie couldn't.

Not with Liam, she couldn't.

Despite her doubts, however, his hand kept moving, creating a wild tempest in her body, his mouth kept burning her lips and neck and breasts, and she was falling…falling. She struggled for a thread of reason in the midst of flooding pleasure.

"No, Liam…wait," she managed to whisper next to his mouth. Despite her words, she shaped his lips to hers feverishly.

"I don't care about our families, Natalie. I don't care about the past. Nothing matters right now but this."

"No…it's not that," she whispered. She clutched desperately to his shoulders and arched against his hand. The need for release from this delicious, mounting pressure nearly ruled her in that moment. It *would* rule her. She couldn't seem to stop it—

"It's just…I've never really done this before."

She barely noticed his mouth pausing against the throbbing pulse at her neck. Pleasure loomed like a wave about to crash over her.

It did.

She couldn't control it. Her body shook at the impact, bliss shooting through every nerve and muscle. She distantly heard Liam say her name, and then he was using his right arm to roll her on her side. He held her against him, as though he used his body to buffer her in a storm, helping her absorb the shock of her pleasure. She pressed tightly to him, needing his strength as she rode the waves of an uncertain ecstasy.

She opened her eyelids a moment later, her body still zinging with aftershocks of pleasure. Liam straightened slightly, looking down at her. He felt hot next to her—hot and very aroused. It took her a moment to focus on his face. His goatee looked dark in the dim room, outlining the grim set of his mouth.

"What did you mean?" he asked.

Her breath froze on a pant. She had no doubt to what he referred. Vulnerability oozed up, breaking through the surface of her dazed consciousness.

"I...I meant I've never been with a man," she said in a cracking voice when she noticed that his rigid expression didn't break.

"Why not?"

Her mouth fell open. She shrugged helplessly.

"The right opportunity just never came up."

Her cheeks heated in rising embarrassment when he continued to stare down at her. She'd thought about telling him the truth ever since he'd first mentioned he wanted to make love to her, but she'd never imagined telling him at such a charged, intimate moment.

She closed her eyes. He must think she was a freak of nature. A virgin...at her age.

"I know it must seem strange to you," she whispered through lips that still felt swollen from Liam's kisses. "But after the crash—once I got out of the hospital and went back to school—everything was different for me." She opened her eyes. A rising sense of trepidation grew in her when she noticed the hint of bewilderment in his eyes. How could she make him understand, when she'd hardly put the experience into words herself? It was just part of the air she breathed, those lonely years of her adolescence, daily feeling her difference in comparison to the children and young adults that surrounded her.

She licked her lower lip nervously when Liam didn't respond. She sensed he was listening, however, with a tight focus, so the words continued to spill out of her as if a pressure valve had been released.

"I was a year behind in school because I'd spent so much time recovering in the hospital," she continued in a cracked voice. "The friends that I'd had moved ahead of me, and I didn't know anyone from the lower grade. That was bad enough. Add to it that Harbor Town is so small. All the kids knew what happened to me. They were cautious. They were curious, too…about the scars. They were actually worse when I was younger. I had a few surgeries after I started school again. Most of the kids avoided me. I don't blame them at all—they didn't know how to talk about serious things."

"Most adults don't, either," Liam said suddenly, startling her. She wished she could interpret the expression on his face. Disappointment swooped through her, so strong it felt akin to nausea when he released her. He pulled the blanket around her, covering her, before he flung his long legs over the side of the bed. Natalie watched in growing helplessness as he remained there, seated at the edge of the mattress with his elbows on his knees and his forehead pressed against his hand.

"And it just kept going?" he asked after a moment. "You were what—twelve years old when you went back to school? Are you saying that people continued to avoid you?"

"Not completely, of course not," Natalie murmured. Was that anger she heard in his voice? She pulled the comforter up higher over her chest, feeling awkward in the knowledge of her nudity. "I made a few friends. But things have a sort of domino effect. Because of what happened to me when I was young, I became known as the shy girl, I guess. The quiet one…the different one." *The scarred one,* Natalie added in the privacy of her mind. No reason to state the obvious. "The girl nobody ever asked out on a date," she finished with a self-conscious laugh.

His head turned sharply.

"That's the most…" He paused, his mouth shaping into a frown that made it look like he wanted to spit something out in furious disgust. "Infuriating thing I've ever heard. How could people be so insensitive?"

She exhaled in relief when she understood the reason for his anger.

"It's only natural, Liam," she said softly. "It just seems strange to you. You were the captain of the football team. You were the homecoming king."

"What the hell has that got to do with anything?" he asked, his bewildered expression telling her loud and clear she might as well have just told him the moon was made of green cheese.

"You lived in a different world than I did during your teenage years. Think about it—if we'd been in the same year at school, would you have sought me out as a friend?"

He looked mutinous. "Of course I would have."

She smiled, grateful to him for his indignation. "You're just saying that because we both were affected by the crash. That made you see the world a little differently than a typical teenager. I should have included in the hypothetical question that you weren't involved in any way in the accident. Would you have wanted to hang around me then?"

He opened his mouth but then paused. Something flickered across his features. He turned his head.

"I was an idiot when I was teenager, especially before the crash. I didn't take anything seriously. It's not fair to judge me based on that."

"I'm not judging you, Liam, that's the point," Natalie said earnestly. "I don't judge any kid for being a kid. It's their right to live in an uncomplicated, happy world and want to stay there."

"You were a kid, too," he said stiffly. "You deserved that as well."

Natalie wasn't sure how to reply. She hadn't been sure what to expect from Liam at her admission, but it certainly hadn't been this frothing, simmering anger.

Her heart froze in her chest when he stood abruptly.

"I'll be right back. Do you want some cold water?"

Natalie just shook her head, feeling as stupid as if he'd just asked her a complicated scientific question.

When he came back carrying a bottle of water, she was standing next to his bed, hurriedly fastening her shorts. He stopped at the door.

"What are you doing?" he asked.

Leave it to her to make a supremely confident man like Liam Kavanaugh look bewildered so many times in one night. Yet…he was the one who had pulled away from her. He was the one who had walked out of the room.

"Nothing," she said, glad to hear her voice sounded even enough. "Just getting dressed." She'd never felt so awkward in her entire life, and Lord knew she'd had her share of uncomfortable moments.

"Well…maybe we'd better…" She waved lamely at the door. If the earth couldn't oblige her by cracking open and swallowing her whole at that moment, the best she could do was exit Liam's bedroom as soon as possible.

"What…you want to leave?"

She barely suppressed a groan that would have told everything she was experiencing at that moment: embarrassment, hurt, confusion, regret.

"I'm not sure what I'm supposed to want, Liam. Or think. You just walked out of the room," she added with more heat than she intended when he just gaped at her.

He winced and set the bottle of water on the bedside table. He came toward her, took her in his arms. Natalie remained stiff in his embrace, her mind churning out anxious thoughts at record high speeds.

"I'm sorry. I'm sorry, Natalie," he spoke roughly near her ear. "I was just…trying to get ahold of myself. I needed a second. I didn't mean to make you feel like I didn't want to be with you. I meant what I said earlier. I want you to stay here. With me."

"You were put off. You were disgusted by what I told you," she said in a pressured rush at the same time that tears leaked beneath her clamped eyelids.

"No. *No*." He pulled her over to the edge of the bed and urged her to sit next to him. His palm cupped her jaw, tilting her face up to him. "I was just trying my damndest to compute what you told me, while still wanting you so bad it was cutting at me at the same time."

She stared at him in amazement, tears still running sluggishly beneath her glasses and onto her cheeks.

"I can't believe you went through all that. It's not fair. I feel like beating the crap out of something…out of someone," he bit out, his jaw tight.

"Liam," she whispered, "I'm okay. I'm all right. I was just trying to explain to you. I'm not really used to talking about it. I've never *had* to talk about it before."

He looked troubled.

"What's wrong?" she whispered, not understanding the source of his unrest, but sensing the depth of it.

He didn't respond for a taut moment.

"I'd like to kill my dad at the moment, if he wasn't already dead."

She inhaled sharply at the impact of his stark words. For a blinding second, she considered what it would be like to say something similar about her mother to another person. The thought horrified her. This thing she'd started with Liam had the potential to hurt so many people…. She placed her fingertips briefly on her eyelids and felt the burn.

"Don't say that, Liam."

"Why? It's the truth. He's the one who did it. He's the one who took away your childhood. My own father." He gave her a wild glance. "It's like…I knew that before, but I didn't *know* it. That sounds stupid, but it's true," he mumbled under his breath.

"No. It doesn't sound stupid. I understand," she assured him. She looped her arms around his waist in a comforting gesture. "Derry made a mistake. It affected a lot of lives. If I could have explained to you why I'm a virgin in a way that didn't involve the crash, I would have. But for me, that's where it all started. Who knows? Maybe I would have been this socially backward if the accident never occurred. I was certainly shy enough—"

"You don't believe that," Liam said with quiet bitterness.

"No. I don't," she admitted. She inhaled slowly. What a mess this was. "I guess this is one of the primary reasons why it's a bad idea for us to get involved."

"Hmm?" he asked distractedly.

"There's too much between us. The closer you get to me, the more you might come to resent your father's memory. I don't want that for you."

"You don't need to take on the worry of what I think of my father," Liam said in a hard tone. "That's not your responsibility. If I want to be with you, then I'll be the one to deal with that."

Natalie looked up at him. "*If* you want to? Does that mean you haven't decided?"

His fierce expression faded. His thumb brushed against her cheek softly. "It means I'm starting to realize it was a bigger decision than I'd been imagining."

Her heart seemed to drop when she heard that. So...she hadn't been too wrong when she'd thought that making love was much more of a simple, mundane occurrence to him than it would have been to her. Now that he fully understood all the baggage that might come along with their intimacy, he obviously was losing interest.

Surprise, surprise.

"Don't, Natalie," he warned softly.

"Don't what?" she asked, wondering what he'd spied on her face.

"Don't think that I'm not making love to you right this second because I find you lacking in any way. You think you've led a secluded life so far. If you had any idea how sexy I think you are, you'd probably run out of this house and begin a life of isolation in earnest," he added under his breath wryly.

Laughter burst out of her throat. He smiled at the sound.

"I guess you probably think I'm a real idiot, for not really getting how complicated this situation was for you," he said.

"I don't think you're an idiot. And it's complicated for both of us," she whispered.

"I just need to absorb it all, that's all. I don't want to screw this up."

She nodded. "I understand."

He grimaced and grabbed a handful of her loose hair, seeming distracted as he let the length run through his fingers. "I kind of doubt you do, actually, since I'm not so sure I understand myself." His head came up. "Do you think it's selfish of me to ask you to sleep here tonight? Just to sleep. I meant what I said before—maybe I mean it more now. I don't want to take you back to your place, but I will, if you want me to."

"I don't know, Liam," she said doubtfully. "I don't think that'd be a very good idea."

He nodded. "Okay."

"I mean…what would the *point* of that be? Me sleeping here?" she asked impulsively.

He shrugged. "Beyond my selfishness in wanting you near me, you mean? No point, I guess. It just…seems right," he said slowly. "It seems like you should be here." When he saw her indecision, he stood, her hand in his. "Come on. I'll show you the guest room. It's not as nice as I want it to be, but it's getting there. You can decide after you see it."

Natalie chuckled, but she let him lead her out of the room. She was so bowled over by the events of the evening that laughing seemed like her only viable reaction.

Either laugh or cry…

"My decision has nothing to do with how nice the guest room is, Liam," she chastised as they walked down the hall, hand in hand.

"And here's the guest bath," Liam said thirty seconds later as he leaned into a doorway and flipped on a light. "There's a couple new toothbrushes and other stuff you can use here in the drawer."

"I can't believe how much you've done to it," Natalie said in amazement as she inspected the fully decorated guest room, complete with fresh pale blue paint on the walls, white wainscoting and trim and what looked to be brand-new fluffy bedding ensembles on the twin beds. Two matted and framed watercolors of sailboats hung on the wall. All was fresh and as pristine as Lake Michigan itself on a sunny morning. "Why did you do the guest room before your own bedroom?"

He shrugged. "I don't care about how quickly stuff gets done for myself, as long as I have a bed to sleep in. But my niece and nephew—Brendan and Jenny, Colleen's kids—are all excited to come and stay, so I had to get things ready for them."

Natalie smiled as she sat down in the cushioned wicker chair next to the window. It filled her with warmth to think of him setting that priority, to consider Liam working so hard to complete a space where his family could come and visit.

Surely her instincts were good when it came to him. Their situation may be strange and emotionally volatile…

But *Liam,* she trusted.

She realized she should have been put off by the fact that

he'd stopped making love to her, confused by his actions. Instead, she understood his ambivalence about plunging into a love affair, because she shared in it. Somehow, it felt all right to move cautiously.

At least to sleep on things.

Besides, it'd be living out a childhood fantasy to spend the night in the Myerson cottage.

"Okay. I'll stay," she said.

His head swung around.

"You will? Just like that?" he asked.

Natalie nodded, thinking of how they'd both just acknowledged how complicated things were between them. And yet, what was life without the occasional risk?

"Yeah," she replied, a smile shaping her lips as she registered Liam's pleased expression. "Just like that."

Chapter Ten

He couldn't sleep for hours, thinking about the investigation and what he'd learned that day about his father.

But mostly, he couldn't find rest because he kept replaying in his mind what had happened in his bed with Natalie earlier—what she'd told him about being made into an outcast by her peers after the accident, the fury he'd experienced at the full comprehension of her suffering…

What it felt like to hold her in his arms while she shook in pleasure.

That was definitely the memory that made him lose the most sleep.

He wanted her in a way he'd never wanted another woman. The knowledge that she slept just feet away from him both tortured him and calmed him at once. The paradox only made sense in light of his self-doubt. What he'd said to her earlier was true. He really did get an odd sort of satisfaction about Natalie being there in the house with him. His desire to make love to her was equally as strong, as natural and essential as the need to draw breath.

The truth she'd revealed hurt, though. It made him realize how selfish he was being for saying their pasts didn't matter. His father had already caused Natalie a lifetime of pain. How fair was it for him to risk hurting her more, all because he couldn't stop wanting her?

Might as well face it—Natalie Reyes was a beautiful, desirable woman. She was also unlike any other woman he'd ever been with. She was different...on so many levels. Liam had a feeling how he handled this situation was a test of his character, and he was suddenly afraid he was going to fail.

His doubt and fear had him tossing and turning until three in the morning. He lectured himself on the necessity for restraint, schooled himself to strike the right note with Natalie between caution and warmth. By the time he fell asleep to the sound of a summer storm, he was sure he'd taken command of his unruly desires.

He was sure, that is, until he woke up to a room filled with pale gold sunlight, his mind sharp and focused on the target of Natalie resting down the hallway, his body rigid and aching with desire.

He stood and threw on a pair of jeans. He'd just look at her while she slept. That's all he planned to do, he promised himself.

He pushed open the guest room door and saw the empty, made beds. He charged down the hallway.

Where had she gone? Had she changed her mind about staying with him and walked home?

Some instinct made him swerve off target and enter the empty upstairs room—George Myerson's old saloon. For a moment he stood motionless at one of the windows, watching as Natalie paused in the shallows of the lake, gathering her long, unbound hair and restraining it at her neck. Her movements held him spellbound. He recalled how he'd been so entranced by her hands when he'd first seen her dancing on the beach.

She began to walk deeper into the water. Her rib cage and waist were so narrow, so graceful…such a striking contrast to her feminine hips. He recalled in graphic detail what those curves felt like filling his palms.

Idiots. All those guys her age must have been witless fools not to see how beautiful she was…how glorious.

He turned and left the room, determination and desire hastening his steps.

The dawn-chilled water provided the brisk slap of distraction Natalie required. She'd slept solidly for five or six hours, strangely content in the embrace of the quiet old house. She'd awoken early, though, and fallen prey to her worries.

Not to mention her memories.

Those things Liam had whispered roughly in her ear last night while he'd played her flesh like a maestro—illicit things, exciting things…but sweet things, as well.

So sweet.

Every recalled word was like a heated touch as she lay there, alone and sweating in bed.

She'd crept downstairs to find her swimsuit. The frigid lake water would help her to quench the burning in her body.

It took her a moment to realize that a current had caught her as she swam. She straightened in the water and tried to break free of the push of the flowing undertow while treading water. A cry of frustration left her throat when she realized the current was stronger than she was. She'd been caught in a current a few times and knew she wasn't supposed to fight it. The force of the water usually diminished after a short span.

The only problem was, the current was carrying her at

a surprisingly fast pace toward the old, jagged breakwater. Natalie saw that a portion of the rock embankment seemed to have fallen during the night. The waves surging fast and furious through the opening in the wall appeared to be what was causing the unusually strong current.

She remained calm, even as she swooped toward the wall, unable to control her movement except to keep her head above the churning water. She suspected the worst that would happen was a cut or a bruise as her body struck the rocks, but then she'd be able to push off the solid barrier and break free of the current.

Her concern grew, however, when she felt the fierceness of the flowing undertow as she flew toward the black, slick rocks. They looked sharper the closer she got. An alarm went off in her brain for the first time when another current seemed to join the one that held her prisoner from another direction, increasing the force of the surging water.

A wave of water splashed into her face, making her sputter for air. She should never have swum alone. Hadn't she known since she was a child that it was dangerous to do so?

Distantly, she thought she heard someone calling her name, but the water was rushing around her now. Only frothing water and the black rocks set against a bizarrely benign-looking blue sky existed in her vision. She tried to lift her legs in preparation to catapult off the rocks, but the current held them as if in a vise. Terror pierced her consciousness. Water filled her mouth and she barely had the wherewithal to spit it out as she braced for the crush of the rocks.

Suddenly hands wrapped around her ribs. For a split second, her motion in the strong current eased and then came to a halt. Water still rushed around her body, but the hands held her in place.

"Liam," she sputtered, glancing wildly to the left and seeing him, his head wet and his face rigid with strain. For a frightening second, the current took hold again. She sensed him recoil, and knew he'd hit the rocks, and then they were shooting through the water in the opposite direction of the crumbling breakwater.

"I was just…an undertow caught me…thought I'd…" She paused, coughing when they came to a stop. He still held her while Natalie treaded water feebly, trying to catch her breath. Liam had sprung them out of the undertow, she realized, by allowing his feet to crash against the breakwater and kicking, propelling himself and grabbing Natalie out of the powerful current.

After a moment, her breathing became more regular.

"I'm okay," she muttered, taking in Liam's expression fully for the first time. His face was fixed and anxious. "Thank you so much. I thought I could push off the rocks, but the current was so strong. I wasn't sure I could lift my legs and…"

"Shh," he hushed, his hands shifting on her back and waist. "Don't talk right now. Are you okay? Can you swim, or do you need me to carry you?"

"No. I'm okay. I can swim."

"Show me," he said, releasing her.

He treaded water as he watched her, his anxiety so palpable she never thought to argue with him. She began to swim to shore. Every time she turned her head to breathe, she saw him swimming next to her, his face above water. His blue eyes remained pinned to her, so luminous and fierce in the morning sunlight, it made Natalie feel as if she was being accompanied by a sea-dwelling sentinel sent to guard her.

Her legs felt a little rubbery from fear once they reached the beach, but other than that, she was fortunate enough to be left unscathed. They sat on a large rock together for nearly a minute, neither of them speaking as Natalie's breath calmed.

"Thank you, Liam."

"Don't thank me," he replied gruffly. "I had no idea that breakwater was unsafe. You could have drowned."

"But I didn't." She reached out and touched his upper arm in reassurance. "I think part of the breakwater crumbled last night during the storm. The waves are especially rough today. The combination must have caused the undertow."

"Yeah," Liam said soberly, his narrowed gaze on the black breakwater. "And to think…I was going to let Brendan and Jenny swim out there."

"You wouldn't have let them swim alone. It was my fault. I shouldn't have gone out on my own."

"Let's get you inside," he said, tight-lipped. He stood and helped her rise. Her hand still felt a little shaky, but Liam's hold was steady and warm.

Once they were inside, he handed her an enormous robe and a fluffy towel and urged her toward the guest bath.

"Take a hot shower. You're trembling. It must be shock."

"I'm fine, really," she insisted. Still, she followed Liam's instructions. He looked so worried, she didn't have the heart to argue.

In the shower a few minutes later, she had to admit he might have been right about the shock. It wasn't a chill making her shake. The memory of the strong undertow pulling her seemed more frightening in recollection than it had when she'd been so preoccupied with keeping herself afloat.

By the time she got out of the hot shower, she felt much steadier. She grinned when she inspected the robe Liam had given her. It was made of dark blue cotton, and still had the tags attached. Natalie wondered if his mother had given it to him as a gift. Whoever had provided it wouldn't have had a lover's sensitivity and must not have recognized that Liam wasn't the type to wear robes and slippers.

Liam was clearly most comfortable in his own skin.

A lover's sensitivity.

The phrase came back to her as she brushed her teeth. Is that what she possessed toward Liam? A lover's sensitivity?

She was in the process of working a tangle out of her long, wet hair when a brisk knock at the door startled her.

"Can I come in?" Liam asked from the other side.

"Oh…yes."

The door swung open. Natalie gulped when she saw he wore just a pair of dark blue cotton drawstring pants. They hung so low on his narrow hips she couldn't help but speculate that he wasn't wearing anything under them. He must have just showered as well; his short, wavy hair was still damp and mussed, and she caught a hint of his fresh, spicy scent.

He looked so beautiful to her, standing there in the doorway, so present…so vibrant, that the image struck her consciousness like a gong, leaving her entire body vibrating with awareness.

"Are you doing okay?" he asked.

She nodded and attempted a smile as she held up a snarled tress and the hairbrush. "It can be a pain sometimes," she said breathlessly, referring to her hair.

"Let me."

She just stood there stupidly at the sound of the two words. He came behind her and removed the brush from her clutching hand. Natalie watched him in the mirror, but she would have known precisely what he was doing in those taut moments whether she saw him with her eyes or not, she was so keyed in to him. He was a head and a half taller than her, but he bent his neck, bringing his face close, as if he wanted to inhale her scent. He attended to his task with more careful deliberation than a detective handling evidence at a crime scene. She was highly aware of his body ghosting hers as he moved, adjusting himself to the angle of each new tress. Every time he gathered a new bunch of hair in one hand, a fresh ripple of excitement coursed from her skull to her neck to her breasts.

By the time he detangled the last locks, her entire body was tingling with awareness.

He set down the brush on the counter, the sound of hard plastic hitting marble seeming unnaturally loud in the still room. Without speaking, he gently gathered the damp tresses in his hands, smoothing each hair away from her face. Distantly, Natalie realized there was no veil for her scars, no glasses, no dim light, not even her hair to cloak her.

She didn't care. She was too enthralled with the image of Liam's eyes—how could they look so fierce and so tender at once? She thought for sure her heart would swell past the capacity of her rib cage when he began to slowly wind the thick tail of her gathered hair around one large hand. His palm turned and turned, the dark brown, sleek skein wrapping around his hand and wrist. The movement hypnotized her.

He finally stopped when his hand was against her nape. Natalie stood there, expectant…breathless. He tugged slightly and her head fell back an inch. Their eyes met in the mirror.

"I was a fool," he said.

"When?"

"For not finishing what we started last night."

Her lower lip trembled, but her eyes never wavered from his stare.

"You…you won't regret it?"

He pulled again with his hand, very gently, until she backed against the length of his body. She could feel him perfectly through the thin fabrics covering their nakedness. He lowered his head so that his breath tickled her exposed ear when he spoke.

"I would regret it for the rest of my life if I didn't." His eyes found hers in the mirror again, hot and entreating. "Tell me you trust me. I need to hear it."

"I trust you," she replied without hesitation.

"I might be acting selfishly."

"If you are, so am I, because I want you so much it hurts," she whispered.

He released her hair and turned her, his arms surrounding her. He claimed her with his kiss...ravaged her...cherished her.

He did all of that and more, and Natalie reciprocated with her own brand of desire unleashed.

She moaned into his mouth when he placed his hands on her buttocks and lifted her, raising her to his kiss. Her legs encircled his hips, her heated blood and melting flesh making the intimate gesture seem as natural as breathing. She clung to his shoulders when he moved, their kiss continuing, their hunger mounting.

He took her to his room and laid her on the bed, sitting beside her. His mouth moved, detailing the line of her jaw, sipping at her parted lips. His long fingers gently caressed her neck and collarbone, creating an anguished sense of anticipation to build in her.

"Liam," she murmured, longing roughening her voice. She encircled him with her arms, her fingers running over sleek, dense muscle gloved in thick skin. She pressed her palms flat against his lower back, one hand on either side of his spine, and slid her fingers beneath the elastic band of his pajama bottoms. He groaned at the caress and shifted his weight, coming down next to her on the mattress. It was the license she needed.

Her hands lowered. She held curving, dense muscle and molded it to her palms.

Liam made a strangled sound and his hand flew to the sash of her robe. He made short work of loosening it as he pressed quick, hot kisses to her neck and ear. His whiskers occasionally scraped her sensitive skin, making her shiver with pleasure, but his warm, gifted lips always followed to soothe her.

He lifted his head and watched himself part the fabric of her robe. She caught a glimpse of his rigid features before he lowered his head, pressing his mouth to her belly. She gasped, her hands flying to his head, her fingers twining in his thick, damp hair. His hands smoothed down the sides of her torso, pausing in the caress to lift her to his mouth. His head moved. He covered her belly and ribs with burning kisses and small, tender bites that left her gasping and her flesh tingling.

Natalie felt herself melting into the mattress, melting beneath Liam's stroking hands and hungry mouth. Her breasts thrust upward, her nipples pulling tight in pleasure. His hands shifted to her back and he raised her farther, her back arching off the bed. She cried out in pleasure when his mouth transferred to her breasts. Her sex clenched tight with rising need as he rained kisses over sensitive flesh and then slipped a nipple between his lips.

He drew on her so sweetly, Natalie's plea was almost harsh.

He rose over her at the sound, a long leg covering one of hers, his ribs pressed against her own. He untied the drawstring of his pants. She could feel his lungs working as he panted nearly as rapidly as she did. She felt the remaining barrier of his thin pants fall away, and he reached for the bedside table and found a condom. Wariness flickered through her for a brief few seconds as he put it on, but then Liam lowered over her. He seized her mouth with his own, and smooth, warm, naked skin glided against her tingling flesh in a caress that struck her as divine.

Then she was kissing him back and her hands were worshipping him, her desire every bit as intense as his.

She felt him move, steely male strength against her female

softness. He pressed against her and she felt a shock go through his body. She gritted her teeth against a stab of discomfort.

He lifted his head and she saw the look of anguished restraint on his face. She reached for him, tracing his smooth goatee with stroking fingers, wishing she could ease the agony so that only the pleasure remained. Her longing only increased when she realized he probably desired something similar for her.

"It's okay, Liam. It's okay," she whispered.

He opened his mouth as if to speak, but no words came. He flexed his hips, wincing before he dropped his head, bracing himself on his arms. Natalie remained frozen for a moment, trying to accustom herself to the sensation of being filled with Liam, of his flesh fusing with her own.

It was strange.

It was…amazing.

She became aware of his heaving ribs. He lay over her, his arm muscles bulging hard and tight as he held himself off her chest.

She began to burn where they were joined.

She shifted her hips, requiring friction to alleviate the pressure growing in her. Liam groaned gutturally and looked up. She licked her upper lip and tasted sweat.

"I'm sorry," he mumbled almost unintelligibly.

"Don't be."

His throat convulsed. "I don't want to hurt you," he croaked, as if he didn't know which sensation to respond to.

"Liam?"

"Yes?"

"Move. *Please*," she implored.

A wild gleam shone in his eyes. He flexed his hips and she gasped. When he paused, thinking she was uncomfortable, Natalie placed her hands on his buttocks and guided him.

His grunt sounded incredulous...wild.

Feeling him move in her was a miracle. Natalie focused on the sensation to the exclusion of all else. Her entire world narrowed to Liam stroking her as she held him in her deepest embrace. She moved with him, knowing this dance instinctively, recognizing this partner at her very core.

When she sensed his tension and heard his erratic breath, she positioned herself to take him deeper, wanting nothing more than to offer him surcease.

"Natalie," he rasped. He lowered his head, his mouth finding hers as they continued to move in tandem. His possession became more demanding, more frantic. His lips moved against her temple, his breath hot and ragged. Natalie closed her eyelid and felt his kiss on her scar like a benediction conferred in fire.

He gave a low, desperate sounding growl and covered her mouth. She felt him jerk within her, his entire body convulsing. The sensation made a flame rage into an inferno. She clutched his shoulders as she succumbed to the unbearable friction Liam created with every look, every touch, every stroke.

His groan of release penetrated her wave of pleasure, striking her as poignant, beautiful—the essence of male surrender.

Chapter Eleven

They lay so entwined Natalie wasn't sure where he began and she ended.

"Are you sure you haven't done this before?" he asked as he kissed her ear. She shivered at the sensual impact of his deep, rough voice.

"Quite sure."

"Huh," he muttered, now kissing her neck with warm lips. "You come by it naturally. How lucky am I? Hey—" His lip examination of her throat broke off when she swatted him on the rear. It was the natural thing to do, since her hand was right there. "It was just an observation."

Natalie grinned as she examined his mussed hair, the shadow of whiskers on his jaw and the humor in his eyes. He looked good enough to eat. She shook her head in admonishment.

"Don't give me that innocent look," she murmured.

"What?" he asked in a low growl. He bent his head and

spoke next to the upper curve of her breast. "The days of being businesslike are done. Now you have to put up with me saying all kinds of unprofessional things. Hmm...." He trailed off as his lips ran over her skin. "I can't believe how soft your breasts are," he murmured, his teasing tone segueing to one of masculine hunger and awe.

"Unprofessional things like that, I suppose," she said on a sigh of pleasure.

"Yeah, things like that, and things like this—" He lifted his tawny head and whispered hoarsely in her ear. Heat rushed through when she heard those sweet, illicit words. Her cheeks burned. So did other parts of her body.

"I had no idea you were such a dirty talker, Liam Kavanaugh," she murmured, hugging him closer as he began kissing her ear in earnest.

"You haven't heard anything yet."

Natalie chuckled. Her body was responding wholeheartedly to Liam's erotic playfulness. Because they pressed skin to skin, it was pretty obvious he was aroused once again. They'd already made love once after that first time, and it'd been as sweet and tender as their first time had been anguished and wild. From Liam's present actions, Natalie surmised this time was going to be different still. Apparently, Liam's lovemaking had as many faces as his complex character.

His kisses were getting so hungry and hot that Natalie opened her eyes in disappointment when they stopped suddenly.

"What's wrong?" she whispered when she noticed he was staring down at her, his eyes lit like banked flames.

"I think I've put you through enough this morning."

"You make it sound like you were pulling teeth or something. It was hardly grueling," she told him with a grin.

He stared. His body hardened noticeably next to her and

she thought she might have convinced him that she wasn't going to break like glass when he sighed deeply and rolled off her.

Natalie scowled at the absence of his heat. She'd grown quite used to it in the past hour.

"You're pretty convincing, you know that?" he asked gruffly as he grabbed his cotton pants.

"Then why are you getting dressed?"

"Because I was damn well near letting myself believe you, that's why," he mumbled.

"Liam."

He pulled up his pants as he stood. He made an impatient gesture when he heard her scolding tone.

"I may not have much experience with…being with someone without much experience," he said, "but I do know one thing—only a jerk would overdo it in these circumstances."

"But—"

"Stop testing my better nature," he said teasingly, but she caught the steel in his stare. "You just get dressed and come on downstairs. I'll make you some breakfast, and then we'll go on over to your place to pick up some stuff."

"What sort of stuff?" Natalie asked bemusedly as she sat up in bed, a sheet clutched over her breasts.

"Whatever you need to stay here for the rest of the weekend, of course," he said, his gaze lingering on her scantily covered breasts. "I may be cutting you some slack because of the special circumstances, but you better believe after you're rested and fed, you're not leaving that bed for a few days."

Natalie stared after him incredulously, but she was laughing by the time she heard his buoyant-sounding tread on the stairs.

Later that afternoon they lay sprawled on recliners on the sunny portion of Liam's terrace. Natalie's skin had dried from their swim and she was getting drowsy from the pleasant feeling of the warm sun. Liam had insisted earlier they stay in the shallows until he had the breakwater repaired, which was fine by Natalie. Not only did she not want to repeat the harrowing experience of this morning, it was much nicer to be in Liam's solid embrace as the waves rushed around their waists. They'd kissed until Natalie was breathless and Liam was so hot, he suddenly fell comically back into the waves, dousing himself.

She felt a little guilty because she hadn't thought once about their investigation into the crash all day.

She'd been too involved with Liam, too preoccupied with observing the way his eyes lit up whenever he heard her laugh, too aware of his every movement, word and touch.

She was falling in love, Natalie realized groggily. It was a little intimidating, not knowing where the path with Liam would end.

His hand grasped hers, as if he'd gleaned her thoughts and was telling her he was on the path with her. She opened her heavy eyelids and smiled sleepily when she saw that while his head rested on the recliner, his chin was tilted and he was watching her.

"Tomorrow is the fundraiser at the Family Center," she murmured, surprising herself a little with her choice of topic. Perhaps her anxieties about becoming involved with Liam weren't as far from the surface as she'd assumed.

"Yeah, but I still have you to myself for the rest of today and all night, so I'm trying not to dwell on having to share you for a while."

She smiled. He returned her smile and caressed her wrist with his thumb. It felt sublime, lying here under a warm sun and having Liam look at her the way he was in that moment. Still…some of her insecurities leaked into her bliss.

"Do you suppose your mother will be there?" she asked slowly.

"She'll probably stop by for a bit. She's still not entirely comfortable with the idea of Mari opening the Family Center, but she does her best to be supportive. Besides, my mom would never miss a chance to spoil her granddaughter," Liam said, referring to Marc and Mari's sixteen-month-old daughter, Rylee Jean.

"Will it be uncomfortable for you? Being there with me?" Natalie asked in a hushed tone.

"I can assure you that being with you makes me *extremely* comfortable."

She threw him an exasperated glance. "I was referring to you being uncomfortable after what happened between you and your mother the other day."

"I know. I'll deal with it. Will it be okay with you?" he asked after a moment. "Your brother will be at the fundraiser as well."

"I can handle Eric. He'll behave," Natalie said quietly. "It's just that…your mother…those things she said to you the other day…"

"You're worried my mother won't behave?" Liam asked with grim amusement.

"I know she'll *behave*." She gave him a furtive glance. "But…if you two have a falling out, it'll have been my fault, for asking you to take on this investigation. I knew that in the beginning, but now…things are different…"

He turned onto his side, facing her. Despite her rising anxiety, she couldn't stop herself from admiring him wearing nothing but some low-riding, black swim trunks.

"Things are different." A small smile flickered across his mouth. "What's different, Natalie?"

She bit at her bottom lip.

"I care. That's what's different."

For a few seconds, he didn't speak. Then he reached for her.

"Come here," he said.

She couldn't resist his beckoning. She laughed after he'd pulled her on top of him and she landed on him in a graceless heap.

"Ouch…hey, watch the elbows," he mumbled as Natalie squirmed, trying to find a comfortable position.

"I'm trying not to crush you."

"You're too small to crush me."

"I'm not too small to break this deck chair," Natalie said, eyes going wide when she heard the springs creak.

Liam's low laugh struck her as delicious. She stopped squirming and rested her head on his warm, hard chest, absorbing the vibrations of his mirth. He smoothed her hair back from her face.

"There. That's better," he said.

Natalie sighed in contentment, sandwiched as she was between Liam's heat and the sun's.

"Listen to me," he said, his deep voice rumbling directly into the ear pressed to his chest. "I can handle my mother, just like you can handle your brother. You weren't wrong to ask me to look into the crash. It's like you told me in the beginning—the truth is what's important."

"Family is important, too."

For a few seconds, she'd wondered if he'd heard her, because he didn't move or respond. She couldn't see him in their present position, but she imagined his expression at that moment—the careworn, sober one he rarely showed the world, the face of a much older man.

Natalie suspected he'd acquired that expression when he was a fifteen-year-old boy.

"You're right. But if family ties are strong enough, they

shouldn't be damaged by the truth," he said before he resumed stroking her hair.

She lifted her head slowly. An ache started up in her throat when she saw he wore the precise expression she'd imagined. A strange sense of foreboding came over her. She'd been the one to suggest this venture because her lack of understanding nettled her so greatly, made it difficult for her to heal.

But what if in finding the answers to the questions that burned inside her, she tore open old wounds for Liam?

What if her questions inflicted new, fresh wounds?

The possibility horrified her.

She opened her mouth to suggest they cease the investigation, but at the same moment he slid her body up farther against his. He lifted his head and took her mouth in a hot, possessive kiss. Her worries fizzled into mist.

He must have known it from years of experience, Natalie thought dazedly.

He must have known it was impossible for a woman to worry and kiss him at the same time.

By the time he sealed the kiss, her flesh had softened to the consistency of warm butter.

"Why don't I take you out to dinner?" he asked gruffly.

"Oh," she mumbled, surprised by his suggestion. "If that's what you'd like to do."

He cradled her jaw with one hand. "What I'd like to do is take you to bed. But I'm trying to restrain the caveman in me—for as long as possible, anyway."

"Liam...I'm fine," she whispered, both embarrassed and pleased by his words.

His hands found their way to her waist. Natalie moaned softly when he lowered to her hips and massaged the flesh there in a hungry gesture. His mouth slanted into a grim line.

"Come on, let's go shower," he said.

He swatted her bottom and she jumped. She glanced up

at him and noticed the gleam in his narrowed eyes. She got off Liam's warm, hard body as if it had just burned her. As she headed toward the back door, she glanced back over her shoulder cautiously. When she saw the devilish expression on Liam's face, she gave a hoot of laughter and started running toward the screen door.

He caught her around the waist just as she reached it and lifted her off her feet. He flung open the door as he held her against him with one arm. His twiddling fingers on her waist and belly made her shriek in surprise. Liam burst into laughter at the comical sound. She couldn't stop laughing as he carried her through the dim kitchen.

"You didn't know cavemen knew so much about tickling, did you?" he teased as Natalie tried to catch her breath between eruptions of laughter.

"Oh…stop, *stop it,*" she pleaded breathlessly as he carried her through the living room.

"If you insist."

She gave one last snort after he'd set her on her feet at the base of the stairs. Her cheeks were wet from laughing. Liam stood just inches away, grinning down at her. She tried to give him a repressive look for tickling her half to death, but he looked so appealing, her pretend irritation couldn't survive.

She grinned back at him as if they were partners in a playful crime.

"I'll get you back for that," she murmured softly.

His eyebrows shot upward. "I can't wait."

"You'll be very, very sorry. You'll see," Natalie told him before she started up the stairs. His deep laughter followed her.

"Natalie," he called.

She paused on the stairs and turned.

"You're the most beautiful thing I've ever seen in my life," he said, his tone completely at odds with their former playfulness.

Her giddy smile vanished. For a few taut seconds, they just stared at each other. The air separating them seemed to pulse with electric tension. Natalie swallowed with difficulty.

"I was thinking…" she began.

"Yes?"

"Maybe we can go to the Captain and Crew for dinner."

His eyes flashed with surprise. What she'd said hadn't been what he'd expected, obviously. She saw his widening smile.

Apparently…he'd liked it, though. He'd liked it a lot.

It was nowhere near as bad as she'd always worried it would be, eating in such a bustling, crowded restaurant in Harbor Town. Natalie knew it was because of Liam. He was a buffer, of sorts. It was hard to worry about judgmental appraisals when she was feeling so happy.

Liam was so well known in town that a few of the bolder Harbor Town citizens initially approached their table. He was never rude—from what Natalie could see, his manners were perfectly amiable. Still, people must have noticed some vibe he transmitted, some signal that he wanted privacy, because no one lingered. They were left to the privacy and wonder of their growing feelings.

"That was nice," Natalie said later when they walked through the door of the cottage. She'd sounded a little breathless. Her sense of anticipation had been mounting ever since their charged encounter on the stairs earlier. It only seemed to build as they had dinner at the Captain and Crew and then took a walk along the harbor.

"You think so?" Liam asked as they walked into the kitchen.

Natalie nodded.

"You seemed relaxed," Liam said. Despite his casual manner, she knew it wasn't an off-the-cuff observation. He'd been watching her with keen attention tonight. Her days of believing Liam was a gorgeous, clueless beachboy were long gone.

"I was. I want to thank you, Liam."

"Why?"

"You were right. I shouldn't let other people rule my actions. I shouldn't…hide."

He came to a stop next to the refrigerator and looked at her.

"You're right. You're the last person on the planet who should ever hide."

She shifted restlessly when she noticed the way Liam was staring at her mouth.

"Do you want anything?" he asked, his stare unwavering. "Some cold water?"

"No. Not cold water."

Her heart started to pound in double-time when Liam didn't move. Something told her he wanted her to go to him, wanted her to make the first move. She stepped forward and looped her arms around his waist.

It might have been the most difficult thing she'd ever done in her life to date. Liam's nostrils flared slightly as he looked down at her, his expression rigid.

"You. I want you." Her voice had never sounded stranger to her own ears and yet…never truer, either.

His pressing body tensed before his mouth swooped downward. Natalie met him halfway for the kiss, feeling a shock go through her at the impact as the coil of their combined restraint sprung free.

His low, vibrating groan thrilled her. His kiss consumed her.

His hands lowered to her hips. He lifted her. She continued to kiss him as if her life depended on that electric, ephemeral thread lacing them together. Her bottom hit the kitchen counter with a gentle thud. He slid her along the slick surface toward him. His mouth felt hot on her throat. His gruff voice penetrated her awareness. He sounded a little desperate.

"Natalie, I want to be careful with you, I want to go easy, but—"

"I don't want easy. I don't want careful. Please don't hold back. I need the opposite from you. I need it *so* much."

It wasn't until that moment she realized it was true. Liam's attraction toward her, his need, had brought her to life somehow…sanctified her.

She seized his mouth with her own. The increasingly familiar fog of sensuality encapsulated her, and she forgot everything but Liam…

Everything but *this*.

Liam threatened to keep her hostage in bed instead of attending the Family Center fundraiser the following afternoon.

"Don't be selfish," she remonstrated as she'd pulled free of his arms, reluctant as she was to do so. "Mari would be disappointed if you didn't go."

"She'd be disappointed if you didn't, as well."

She glanced back at the sound of his low rumble. It'd been nothing less than an amazing experience being intimate with Liam during this sensual feast of a weekend. He was at times a gentle lover, at times demanding…always masterful. Her wholehearted responsiveness amazed her just as much. It was difficult to say who was more pleased by her tendency to lose all self-consciousness when making love: Liam or herself.

He lay there in bed, one arm resting on the pillow behind him. He wore nothing but the leather woven bracelet around his wrist, the heavy-lidded look of a well-satisfied man, and a sheet, which succeeded in covering pretty much nothing.

Her gaze lingered longingly on the expanse of his ridged, sleek torso.

She turned away with difficulty.

"I don't attend these functions, usually. Mari wouldn't miss me, but she'd miss you. So come on, slacker," she teased, pulling on the sheet that barely draped Liam. He leaped out of bed like a lion, nabbed her, and sent her into a fit of laughter.

What'd followed had delayed them getting ready for the fundraiser by a half hour, but Natalie wasn't complaining.

"Liam?" she called as she walked down the stairs after her shower, running a brush through her hair.

She heard him talking in the distance, but it wasn't to her. As she neared the kitchen, she realized he was on the phone. A notebook and his laptop sat before him on the kitchen table. She hesitated in the entryway between the dining room and kitchen, unsure if she should disturb him. He looked up and saw her standing there. He beckoned to her with his hand as he continued to talk.

"You don't need to apologize, Ellen. I just appreciate you calling back. I hope you had a good trip." He gestured to his iced tea with upraised eyebrows while Ellen spoke, but Natalie shook her head and sat at the table across from him. "I figured that as his administrative assistant, you were the best person to ask about anything that stood out as unusual about my dad during those last days."

A few seconds later, Liam ended the conversation and hung up the phone.

"Your father's assistant at Langford?" Natalie asked.

"Yes. I would have talked to her sooner, but she's been on vacation in Italy. She told me that Dad was definitely preoccupied and withdrawn at work the week of the crash. First thing on Tuesday morning, he'd insisted she try to locate an old friend of his—Evan Mulonovic. I kind of remember Mulonovic. He was one of those old friends of my father's whose name popped up once in a while," Liam explained in a distracted manner as he tapped his fingers rapidly on the keyboard of the computer. He paused for a second, his face sober and his blue eyes intent on the screen, before he resumed. "Ellen said she was able to locate Mulonovic and book a lunch meeting for them on that Tuesday."

"That was the day of the crash," Natalie said in a hushed tone.

"Yeah. According to Ellen, my dad went straight to Harbor Town after that lunch. It says here that Dr. Mulonovic was a pediatrician—a pediatric geneticist, to be exact. He worked at Children's Memorial Hospital."

"What, Liam?" Natalie asked when he suddenly cursed under his breath.

"So much for questioning Mulonovic about anything significant during that lunch meeting. It says here he died of a heart attack a year ago."

Chapter Twelve

They discussed the phone call with Ellen on the way to the fundraiser. By the time he pulled into the field designated for parking next to the Family Center, neither of them had made any sense of the puzzling information.

Most of the regular parking lot was being used for other activities for the fundraiser. The sounds of a party reached his ears: music from a small band, children's hoots of laughter, the buzz of conversation. As they got out of the car, Liam saw information booths, an inflatable bounce house, and ring toss and bottle throw for prizes. Colleen had bribed Tony Tejada, Harbor Town's mayor, with the use of her boat for a week in order to get him into the dunking machine. He noticed his nephew, Brendan, wearing swim trunks running fleetly through the grass, only to go down on one hip. Natalie gasped in alarm, but then Brendan glided like a hockey puck on ice for twenty-five feet.

Liam laughed and took her hand. "That was Marc's idea. You can't lose with the kids when you've got a Slip 'N Slide."

Natalie's smile looked a little shaky as she surveyed the crowd. He paused in the parking area and squeezed her hand.

"Do you really want to do this?" he asked her quietly while he examined her reaction.

She looked amazing in a pair of form-fitting jeans and a turquoise tunic that highlighted both her dancer's lithe figure and healthy tan. The breeze blew a tendril of hair on to her cheek. He hooked it with his finger and drew it back. He'd asked her to wear it down earlier when he'd seen her start to twist it into a bun. She'd complied readily enough, but now he was feeling a little guilty for asking. She should have the right to go out into public any way she damn well felt comfortable.

"I'm fine," Natalie replied, sounding a little breathless.

Liam suddenly had an urge to hustle her back in the car and take her back to the cottage, where they could resume their idyllic weekend. He still had about a million things he wanted to discover about her, and he was sure he'd have another million by the time the weekend was through. Every new discovery was magic—like that she loved John Wayne movies, and cheese curls, and that she made the sweetest sigh when he kissed the side of her left knee. When he'd asked her half teasingly, half in total earnest what her best dance move was, she'd laughed and rolled her eyes. When he'd persisted in getting an answer, she'd told him an arabesque, which meant absolutely nothing to him. Upon more wheedling, she'd shown him the position—her body supported on one leg, the other extended behind her as if she did a split in midair.

The woman was amazing.

He was about to suggest they ditch the fundraiser when Mari Kavanaugh approached, looking beautiful in a pink dress and sandals.

"Liam! There you are. I was just telling Tony Tejada you'd be here. He said next year the citizens of Harbor Town could line up and act out their aggression on the new police chief instead of the mayor. He was a bit tetchy when he said it," Mari said.

"A bit wet, you mean," Liam replied with a grin.

Mari stopped dead in her tracks, her brandy-colored eyes going wide when she saw who stood next to him. "*Natalie.* Oh my God!" Mari rushed her for a hug. "I can't believe you came. Oh, I'm so glad."

It both pleased him and made feel a little sad to see how surprised Mari was that Natalie had attended the public event. He realized Natalie hadn't been at the opening ceremony for the Family Center last year. If she had, he would have noticed her.

Simple as that.

Mari backed out of the hug and glanced dubiously between Natalie and Liam.

"*What* is going on here?" she asked, half mock-stern and half pleased as punch.

"Come on, Mari. I've never known you to be so slow on the uptake," Liam said as he gave his sister-in-law a kiss on the cheek. He noticed Eric Reyes next to the dunking booth, talking to his seven-year-old niece, Jenny, of all people. Eric had noticed Liam and Natalie's arrival. Liam hoped at the very least that he kept his expression as neutral as Eric's. He didn't want to ruin this for Natalie, especially when she was so nervous about making a public appearance.

"Where's that husband of yours? Already campaigning to be senator?" Liam asked Mari.

Mari looked surprised. "Did Marc tell you about that?"

"No. I have my sources of information," Liam said mysteriously. He noticed Mari's bemused expression, and admitted,

"I actually read about the party showing interest in making Marc their candidate for senator in the *Chicago Tribune*."

"Really? Is Marc going to run for senator, Mari?" Natalie asked in surprise.

Mari shook her head. "No...I don't think so. The party interest came out of nowhere. It's flattering, but he loves his job as a state prosecutor too much. Marc's not going to be at all pleased when you tell him there was mention made of it in the newspaper, Liam. You should tell him about the story going public. He took Rylee into the Center. She was getting fussy in the heat and started squalling so loud she sent a whole flock of sparrows flying out of a tree in terror."

Liam grinned. "That's my girl."

"Oh—hi, Eric! Look who's here," Mari greeted Eric Reyes brightly.

"Is Mom here, Mari?" Liam asked quietly while Natalie and Eric hugged and talked. "I need to have a word with her."

"She's inside with Marc and Rylee. I'm going to take Natalie to show her the fountain," Mari added in a confidential undertone.

He gave her an amused look. "Don't you be harassing Natalie. If you want to interrogate someone about us showing up here together, you can ask me."

"You make it sound like there's something significant to ask about in regard to you two," Mari said.

"Maybe there is."

Something indefinable flickered across Mari's features. He recognized it as concern when she gave Natalie a furtive glance. She grabbed his arm and pulled him several feet away for privacy.

"I hadn't expected this," she said.

"Why?" Liam asked bluntly. He was getting sort of sick of people acting like the idea of Natalie and he together was so bizarre. He recalled his uncertainties on the night before he'd made love to Natalie for the first time, however, and he had to admit…maybe the people who cared for Natalie did have some reason for concern.

Mari bit her lower lip and spoke in a low voice. "You've never been much of a one-woman man, Liam. I'm not criticizing," she said quickly when he opened his mouth to protest. "How you run your love life is your business. It's just… Natalie is very vulnerable…"

"Do you think I don't realize that? Don't worry, Mari," Liam said quietly. "Please."

She studied his face with sharp eyes and smiled. "All right. I won't, if you're sure, and I can see that you are." Turning, she walked back toward Natalie. "I want to show you the fountain," Mari said, taking Natalie's hand in a sisterly gesture. "You haven't seen it yet."

"Will you be okay with Mari for a few minutes while I go speak to my mom?" Liam asked Natalie, his voice low. Eric had turned to talk to Allison Trainer, the manager of the Family Center. Liam thought Natalie's brother might be avoiding him, but he couldn't fault Eric for wanting to maintain peace.

"Of course," Natalie assured.

He had a moment's trepidation at leaving her in a crowd. It was quashed when he saw how comfortable she seemed, chatting with Mari as they walked toward the promontory of the Silver Dune and the memorial fountain Marc had donated to the Family Center last year.

Liam headed toward the Center and his mother, the increasingly familiar combination of dread and determination rising in him.

Natalie left Eric and Mari at the silent auction and went in search of Liam. He'd seemed thoughtful…intense, ever since that phone call from his father's old administrative

assistant. When he'd said a while ago he was going to speak
to his mother, she couldn't help but feel some trepidation.
She didn't want to run into Brigit Kavanaugh necessarily,
but she was concerned enough to go in search of him.

She ran into Marc Kavanaugh carrying his daughter at
the entrance to the Family Center. Liam and his elder brother
looked a lot alike, but she found Marc more intimidating for
some reason.

He stared at her in surprise.

"Natalie? It's so great to see you," Marc said, leaning down
to give her a kiss of greeting. Rylee must have thought she
was undergoing a person-to-person transfer, because she put
her chubby arms around Natalie's neck, and the next thing
she knew, the adorable little girl was in her arms.

"Whoops…sorry. I'm a little worried about her, she's so
shy," Marc said amusedly as his daughter proceeded to stroke
Natalie's hair and stare at her with huge brown eyes framed
by thick, dark lashes.

"Pitty," Rylee said with sober earnestness.

"Thank you," Natalie responded instantly before she
grinned, utterly charmed. "Oh, she's adorable."

Rylee grabbed a fistful of the "pitty" hair and tugged.
Marc was there to unclench the little fist immediately.

"I better take her back before you think she's about as
adorable as Attila the Hun."

"I'm fine," Natalie assured, laughing. But when Rylee went
for another handful of hair, Marc swooped the little girl back
into his arms.

"Are you looking for Liam?" Marc asked.

Something about the way he asked the question made Natalie think Liam had spoken to his brother about her.

"I was, yes," she said.

Rylee waved an arm toward the crowd and said something
that sounded like "Enny."

"He's inside," Marc said a little distractedly as his daughter continued to wave her arm.

"Enny," Rylie repeated more energetically.

"Okay, okay. We'll go find your cousin Jenny. Sorry," he told Natalie. "I'm nothing more than her highness's chariot. I move at her command. It's good to see you here, Natalie."

"Thanks. I'll see you later. 'Bye Rylee."

Rylee watched her with big eyes over her father's broad shoulder as they walked away. Natalie smiled and entered the air-conditioned interior of the Family Center. She couldn't help but think that Marc didn't seem half as imposing or intimidating when he held his daughter in his arms.

Natalie had been inside the Family Center several times to do some bookkeeping and other paperwork. She usually came during regular business hours, so she wasn't used to the silence that reigned at the moment. Now that she'd entered the premises, she started to realize how intrusive it might seem for her to interrupt Liam and his mother. She paused in the hallway, feeling uncertain. She started when Liam spoke, his voice much closer than she'd expected.

"You knew him, didn't you? You knew Lincoln DuBois."

Her heart seemingly leaped into her throat when a closed office door just three feet away from her jostled in the catch, as if someone had just leaned on it…or placed a hand on it, preventing it from opening?

"Don't walk away," she heard Liam's quiet voice warn.

"Who do you think you are, asking me these questions?" Brigit Kavanaugh spoke for the first time, her voice cold with fury.

"I'm your son. I'm Derry's son, too. And I have every right to ask about Lincoln DuBois after seeing Dad's reaction to him on that videotape. DuBois grew up in South Lake Tahoe. So did you, Mom. You went to the same private high school for two years before grandpa got transferred to Chicago. He's a famous man—a billionaire I don't know how many times over. You'd think you would have mentioned at least once that you went to school together. Are you still going to deny knowing him?"

"I'm not denying anything," Brigit replied.

"So you're admitting you did?" Liam asked slowly. "Why didn't you ever mention it before?"

"Why would I? He means nothing to me. He was a child-hood friend," Brigit spat.

"Why did he mean so much to Dad, then?" Liam persisted.

Natalie had slowly started to back out of the hallway, but her feet kept stalling. She knew she was intruding on a charged, private conversation, but her curiosity seemed to glue her shoes to the floor.

"*Stop* it, Liam. I've told you half a dozen times now that I'm not going to play this game with you. I've never seen you behave this way. You're acting like a spoiled brat."

"You're acting like someone who has a secret," Liam returned so quickly, so coldly, that Natalie's feet came to a dead halt.

The silence that followed was so tense—so awful—that Natalie cringed inwardly.

"What if I do have a secret?" Brigit finally said. "That doesn't mean you have the right to harass me about it. Maybe I'm keeping that secret because you're my son, and I don't want to burden you with it. Do you have so little faith in me? Why would you automatically assume I'm keeping something from my children with malicious intent? Do you really think that poorly of me?"

"I don't think you're being malicious. If you kept some-thing from us when we were kids, I can understand that," Liam replied, sounding vaguely contrite now. "But we're not kids anymore, Ma. If you know why Dad was so upset on the night of the crash, why don't you tell me? You don't have to shoulder the truth alone. At least tell me what Lincoln DuBois has to do with anything."

"Don't talk to me like I'm a criminal, Liam. Do you think the world began on the day you were born? I was young once. I had a life that didn't revolve exclusively around my children."

"Don't try to make me feel guilty," Liam said, his voice once again like steel.

"We all have secrets," Brigit continued as if he hadn't even spoken. "Marc does. You do. Your father certainly did."

"What's that supposed to mean?"

"It's just the truth, Liam. That's what you're so fond of, right?"

Natalie started guiltily from her hyper-focus on the exchange when the door was flung open and suddenly she was face-to-face with Brigit Kavanaugh.

"You," Brigit said softly.

The word seemed to lance straight through Natalie. There was little doubt what Brigit meant, innocuous as her utterance may seem. It'd sounded like a malediction ringing in Natalie's ears. Liam's mother clearly held Natalie responsible for turning her calm family life upside down.

Brigit rushed past her.

A moment later, Natalie heard the front door slam and she was staring at Liam, whose face looked tinged with gray in the dim light.

Natalie stood on Liam's terrace, squinting to make out the shimmering lake. The night was black. Clouds had swept in that evening, obliterating even starshine.

She heard the screen door squeak and close and knew Liam had joined her. Her hands twisted together nervously. They hadn't spoken much since they'd stood in the hallway of the

Family Center. They'd left the fundraiser soon afterward, driven to his cottage and made dinner.

You heard? Liam had asked her as they stood there in the hallway.

Natalie had nodded her head, embarrassed that she'd eavesdropped on something so personal. Liam had just taken her hand and led her out of the building. For the last two hours, she'd still been vibrating with the shock of hearing the encounter. She thought it was similar for Liam, given his absorption and distance.

Now that the shock was wearing off, uncertainty and nervousness were starting to creep into her awareness. Liam's approach from behind her on the darkened terrace only seemed to amplify her anxiety.

Surely she should leave. She'd overstayed her welcome here. Liam had other things to think about. Perhaps even now he was rethinking the wisdom of becoming involved with her—

"Are you wondering why I didn't tell you that my mother grew up in the same town as Lincoln DuBois?"

She inhaled slowly. His voice had resounded from just behind her. Yet he didn't touch her, Natalie realized with a sinking feeling. She sighed and glanced down. After only a few days, she'd become accustomed to Liam's tender caresses. Their absence now seemed telling.

"Why didn't you?" she asked.

"I wanted to ask my mother first. It only seemed fair. In case it didn't mean anything. I was going to tell you, I just wanted to give my mom a chance to give her side first."

"I understand," Natalie said.

He put his hands on her shoulders and urged her to turn. He was a tall shadow looming over her. She couldn't make out his features, but she sensed his intensity.

"Do you?" he asked.

"I've told you before how important I think family is. Of course you wanted to speak to your mother about it before you mentioned anything to me."

"It's got nothing to do with family loyalty," Liam said, a hint of frustration in his voice. "I just…I'm starting to think she's hiding something."

"Then let's stop. Let's *stop,* Liam."

He'd pulled her in contact with his body, so she felt the shock that went through him at her resolute tone.

"How can you say that with so much certainty, when you're the one who started this? Wouldn't you regret it…stopping?"

She put her arms around his waist. "I might regret *not* stopping," she said, her throat thick with emotion. She thought of what she'd told him when she first visited the cottage, here on this very patio where they now stood. She'd told him there was a chance he might love his father more if he knew the truth of what had motivated Derry that night, not less.

After hearing Brigit's and Liam's heated exchange at the Family Center, she was starting to realize just how naive—how selfish—she'd been in saying that.

"I don't want you to get hurt, Liam," she whispered.

For a few seconds he didn't speak. The tension increased in his body. She kept her gaze trained on his shadowed face as if she could read every nuance of his expression, even though the shadows blinded her.

"We're not stopping," he said. "We're not stopping any of it."

His mouth covered hers, and Natalie knew in that second that Liam's passion had captured her soul…ruled it. Her awkwardness, her unanswered questions, her anxieties and curiosity about the crash—all those things had once been sovereign in her mind.

Now they receded to the background, bowing down to a new master.

His hands—half cherishing, half commanding—moved over her body. Her breasts tingled beneath his touch. She arched into him, eager to make his heat her own.

The earlier conflict seemed to have created a pressure in both of them, the type of friction that required release. Her clothes seemed to melt off her beneath his hasty, adroit fingers. He urged her on to the cushioned recliner. She laid back and stared up at the black night sky, puffs of air and moans flying past her parted lips. His hands and mouth seemed to be everywhere at once, seemingly turning her into a single, throbbing nerve ending.

When he settled on her hip bone, treating it to a gentle kiss, Natalie cried out in rising need and reached for him, trying to urge him up to her, begging him silently to quench the fire he'd set in her flesh.

He made a hushing sound and grabbed her wrists, restraining her. His head moved between her thighs.

She keened softly in awe as pleasure flooded her.

Did he know he kissed her very soul?

The sound of the waves hitting the rocks became obliterated by the pounding of her heart. It became unbearable to exist in this taut world of bliss, friction and intimacy Liam built in her. She strained tight in surrender. The explosion of pleasure—of sheer feeling—that detonated in her flesh was so intense, it almost hurt to succumb.

She still was recovering when she felt Liam slide inside her, filling her, stopping only when they were pressed tight, belly to heaving belly.

"Shh, I've got you," he whispered, his voice a rough caress in her ear before he kissed her there. She distantly heard her own whimpers of anguished release still escaping from her throat and realized he'd been soothing her.

Then Liam began to move, and her pleasure-dazed brain once again focused on approaching ecstasy.

* * *

"I'm going to go to Lake Tahoe," Liam said later, his lips lingering to caress her breast after he spoke.

The hair on the back of her neck stood on end when she registered his words. They lay together on the cushioned recliner, their bodies entwined, the perspiration from their heated lovemaking drying on their skin in the gentle breeze. Natalie realized her stroking fingers in his hair had frozen at his statement.

"To talk to Lincoln DuBois?"

She felt his nod. She resumed stroking him, her mind whirring into overdrive.

"I'm going with you," she said, glad at that moment he couldn't see her apprehensive expression because of the darkness.

Once, the truth about the crash had haunted her, eluded her, a hazy outline she could never quite bring into focus. Now Natalie wished she'd never coveted that prize.

What if that elusive truth destroyed the powerful, but still newborn and fragile connection between Liam and her?

Chapter Thirteen

If it weren't for the breathtaking Lake Tahoe scenery distracting her, Natalie might have thrown up. She was glad Liam was driving the car up the curving mountain road that overlooked the topaz blue alpine lake, and not her. He handled the tight curves like a pro. A thought struck her as she stared at the steep drop-off that looked to be only a few skinny feet from the right front tire of the rental car.

"You said your mother grew up in Tahoe. Do you still have family here?"

"Not anymore. My aunt and uncle lived in Incline Village until I was about nineteen, when they moved to Sacramento."

"Did you visit when you were young? I was wondering why you seem so comfortable driving on this road."

Liam gave her a quick glance, his brow furrowed. Natalie barely resisted an urge to shout at him to look back at the road.

"Is my driving making you nervous?" he asked, a grin tickling his mouth.

"Not your driving, no. You seem very confident. It's this road. I mean…maybe you can't see it, but there's like a hundred foot drop about two inches away from my door," she said, glancing anxiously out the passenger window.

Warmth spread inside her when he started to laugh, a light-hearted sound she hadn't heard from him for several days. In many ways, they'd grown closer in the past week, spending quiet time together, swimming in the continued warm summer weather, taking walks or just sitting on the terrace, always touching, as if they wanted to know the other was there in some tangible sense. He was always warm and considerate with her; he was a great deal more than warm in bed.

But in many ways, she couldn't help but feel he'd grown distant since that night at the fundraiser. He seemed as if he was constantly trying to work out some kind of puzzle in his head. Over the past few nights, she frequently saw him on his computer. On several occasions she heard him talking on the phone in the distance. He'd spent the duration of the flight from Detroit to Reno working, looking over his notes with a sober expression of concentration.

So his deep, earnest laughter filling the interior of the car sounded especially wonderful to her at that moment.

"I've driven this road maybe a dozen times or more in a car, but my cousins and I have circled it a hell of a lot more in dirt bikes."

Natalie gasped. "I can't believe your parents let teenagers on this road on *dirt bikes*."

Liam chuckled. "People in the area don't think of this road like you do. Most residents could drive it in their sleep. If you saw some of the mountain paths my mother used to take on horseback, you'd realize this road is a cakewalk."

At the mention of his mother, his grin flattened.

"Liam...how do you think we should try to get in to see Lincoln DuBois? Should we try and call when once we check into the hotel? I can't imagine he has a number listed publicly, a man like him."

"I have both his address and phone number."

Natalie looked at him in surprise. "How'd you get those?"

"Detectives have their ways."

She laughed. "Apparently."

He shrugged. "It's why you initially hired me, right?"

She wanted to blurt out that a lot had changed since she'd given him a check to investigate his own father, but she figured now wasn't the time to broach that sensitive topic.

"So, how *are* we going to proceed?"

"We're going over to DuBois' place and ask him if he knows anything that might be relevant about my parents and the crash."

"Just like that?"

He gave her a wry glance. "He's expecting us."

Natalie was so shocked she forgot to clutch at her seat as Liam maneuvered a hairpin turn. "You already spoke to him?"

"I didn't speak to him personally. I talked to a few people, but the guy who is going to get us in the door is the Chief Executive Officer of DuBois—Nick Malone. Malone's not the most welcoming of men, but I suppose crackpots try to wriggle their way into DuBois' presence all the time. We got lucky though. DuBois himself was in the room when I spoke with Malone. The only reason we got a meeting with DuBois was because Malone said my mother's name out loud, and DuBois heard it."

"Your mother's name?" she asked slowly.

"Yeah."

Liam now looked so grim, his former laughter might have been a hallucination.

Natalie didn't really know what to expect in regard to visiting a billionaire tycoon's house. Even though Liam had the lakeshore address, they had to ask for directions a few times, the estate was so secluded by towering pine trees and miles of land. When they finally did find the drive, it was unmarked. They didn't realize it was the road to DuBois estate until they pulled up to the iron gates and saw the numbers for the address innocuously printed in tiny numerals on the metal of the security intercom.

"Malone may have given us the address, but he sure as hell didn't want to make things easy for us to see DuBois," Liam muttered before he pressed the intercom from his car window.

Perhaps a Hollywood influence had her imagining a maid dressed in a black dress and a white apron, so she was a little taken aback when the door to the sprawling house was answered by a cowboy.

Well, not a *cowboy,* really—there was no hat or enormous belt buckle, but the tall, fit man with the wavy chestnut brown certainly looked as if he'd be comfortable in a horse's saddle.

"Can I help you?" he asked, although his clear, cold gray eyes hardly seemed like he wanted to give them assistance.

"We're here to speak to Lincoln DuBois. I'm Liam Kavanaugh. This is Natalie Reyes." Even though she'd seen Liam shake hands with innumerable people in the past several weeks, he didn't offer his hand, which surprised Natalie a little.

For a few seconds, the man didn't say anything. Natalie shifted on her feet uncomfortably when she noticed Liam and the man were having a staring contest.

"We spoke on the phone. I'm Nick Malone."

"I figured you were. I recognized your voice," Liam said so pleasantly it was as if he hadn't noticed the chill in the air, even though Natalie knew for certain he had.

"I don't like this. Mr. DuBois isn't at all well."

"You mentioned that several times on the phone. I promise you we'll be considerate of his health. It was my understanding that it was Mr. DuBois' particular wish to speak with me."

That did it. Nick Malone stepped back, allowing them to enter.

"Follow me," he said.

Malone led them into a truly stunning great room, featuring a forty-foot ceiling and the largest picture window Natalie had ever seen. The house was built on the side of a mountain. Its panoramic view of a sparkling Lake Tahoe and the surrounding High Sierras was the most jaw-dropping she'd ever seen.

They followed Malone up a grand staircase made with lodgepole pines and down a hallway, which was more of a gallery, given the museum-quality paintings hanging on the wall and occasional sculptures.

Nick gave them a severe once-over as he knocked at a door.

"Linc? Are you awake?"

"I am," was the quiet reply.

"Mr. Kavanaugh and Ms. Reyes have arrived."

"Send them in," the voice on the other side of the door came more energetically.

Malone put his hand on the doorknob and turned to Liam.

"He's very frail. His level of awareness wavers, depending on how fatigued he is. Don't badger him with a lot of questions."

Liam smiled even though his eyes were like blue ice chips. "No worries. We'll be very gentle. *My* mother taught me good manners."

Despite Liam's sarcasm, Malone turned the knob and

pushed open the door. He shut it behind them with an angry click once they'd entered the room.

And what a room…Natalie thought in wonder as she looked around the enormous space filled with everything from plush oriental carpets to detailed nautical maps that had been framed and mounted on the wall. Interspersed were oil paintings of horses.

DuBois himself was in the middle of all this wonder, sitting in a wheelchair, his gaze fixed on Liam. He had the look of a man who had lost a great deal of weight in a short period of time, leaving him lined and shrunken. Only his thick, steel-gray hair carried a remnant of former vitality.

"Mr. DuBois? Thank you for seeing us," Liam said warmly, shaking the man's outstretched hand. "This is Natalie Reyes."

"Hello," Natalie said, taking DuBois' frail hand in her own. He nodded courteously at her, but immediately turned his attention back to Liam.

She knew by now that DuBois was only a few years older than Brigit Kavanaugh, but they might as well have been of different generations. Brigit could have passed for a woman in her late forties. DuBois' multiple strokes had taken their toll, however. He might have been in his late seventies instead of in his sixties.

"I thought you might resemble her more," he told Liam in a feeble voice. "I thought you might look more like your mother. Beautiful Brigit."

Liam smiled. "I take more after my father, I'm afraid."

A cloud seemed to fall over DuBois' features.

"I understand you went to school with my mother," Liam said.

"Yes, yes," DuBois said, some of the animation returning to his face. He waved them over to a plush velvet couch. Once they were seated, he maneuvered his chair so that he faced them. "She was my first love, Brigit Darien. You see? There," he said, nodding toward several photographs arranged on a round end table. Liam leaned over and plucked out one frame. He held it in his lap, examining the photograph of what was obviously a teenage Brigit Kavanaugh sitting on the back of a brown horse with a gleaming coat. Brigit looked beautiful, the sunlight making her hair a luminous gold, a brilliant smile for whoever had snapped the photo.

"Brigit practically lived on my father's ranch for a few years. A more natural horsewoman I've never seen. It broke my heart when she moved to Chicago."

"I can see how she would break your heart. She was so pretty," Natalie said. "When did you and Brigit meet?"

"We were both enrolled by our parents at a local stable for lessons. I grew up on a working ranch, and can't even remember when I wasn't riding, but I didn't know anything about showing a horse until I was fourteen or so. Brigit would have been about twelve. She preferred jumping, and I was into roping, but once we got past our prejudices for each other's expertise, we became the best of friends."

Liam chuckled as he returned the photograph to the table. Despite his show of amusement, Natalie sensed his tension. She shared in it.

"You two were close," Liam mused. "I'm surprised my mother has never spoken of you."

"No?" DuBois asked in a quavering voice.

"Well, not much," Liam added quickly when he saw the impact his words had on the frail man. "I suppose that's natural."

"Yes," DuBois said sadly. "She's a married woman, with children of her own."

"You never had children, Mr. DuBois?" Natalie asked.

"Please…call me Linc. No, I never did. One of the biggest regrets of my life," DuBois said with a sad smile. "I've built an empire, but I was too stupid to ever pause and build a family—although Nick is practically a son to me. Still… don't either of you hesitate to start a family if you haven't already. What's the use of all this—" he waved vaguely at the luxurious room "—if you have no one to share it with?"

A pause ensued in which Dubois stared into space blankly. Natalie glanced at Liam.

"Mr. DuBois?" Liam asked gently.

DuBois blinked and refocused on them. For a few seconds, Natalie was quite sure he didn't have any memory of who they were. His illness had clearly affected his mind as well as his body.

"I'm here to ask you about a car crash that occurred sixteen years ago. My father caused that crash. Do you know anything about that?"

DuBois looked completely blank. "Car crash?" he asked slowly. "What car crash? On the lake road?"

Liam inhaled and leaned forward, his elbows on his knees. Natalie thought she understood his cautiousness. DuBois suddenly seemed fatigued and less sharp than he had been previously.

"My father—Derry Kavanaugh—caused the accident. The crash occurred in Michigan, not here in Tahoe. It happened sixteen years ago. Did you ever meet Derry Kavanaugh?"

DuBois just stared back at him, his pale blue eyes blank.

Liam cast a wary glance her way before he continued. "Mr. DuBois…when is the last time you saw my mother, Brigit Kavanaugh? Brigit Darien," Liam added his mother's maiden name quickly when DuBois' expression remained uncomprehending. Although he'd recalled the name Kavanaugh earlier, and seemed to understand who Liam was, the name seemed to mean nothing to him at present.

The name Darien, however, had the effect of hitting a light switch.

Dubois beamed. "On the New Year—1976."

For a few seconds, both Natalie and Brigit stared. The precise, quick response hadn't been what they'd expected.

"You…you remember so well," Liam commented.

"Of course I do," DuBois said matter-of-factly. "How could I forget such a special night with my beautiful Brigit. She came back to me, on that night. I knew that husband of hers couldn't be faithful to her. I knew it,"

Natalie's mouth had gone bone-dry. She glanced anxiously at Liam, who appeared to have been frozen by DuBois' words.

"Mr. DuBois," she began. "I think we've taken enough of your time. You must be very tired—"

"1976?" Liam interrupted her. "Are you saying my mother—Brigit Darien—was with you in 1976? Are you certain?"

"Of course I am, do you think I'd forget a night like that?" DuBois asked. "Brigit was torn to pieces by what her husband had done. Maybe some would say she was just as unfaithful on that night with me, but they'd be wrong. They'd be *dead* wrong," he said so firmly, so fiercely that Natalie had a glimpse of the decisive, charismatic man DuBois must once have been. She stared, anxiety, confusion and horror rising in her in equal measure.

She'd worried they might discover something that would further damage Liam's opinion of his father. Now it seemed this investigation might make him question his mother, as well. Natalie had never felt so helpless in her life. There was nothing they could do to stop it. It was like standing beneath a gigantic avalanche, with nowhere to run.

The truth just kept spilling out of DuBois' mouth.

"Brigit was mine before she was ever that fool's from Chicago. Maybe we only had one night together, but who did she come to in her distress? *Me*."

DuBois' fierceness seemed to leak out of him as quickly as it had come. He sat slumped in his chair, staring at the table where the young, beautiful girl sat smiling on the horse, her image frozen in time.

"Brigit had a baby nine months after that. A mutual friend who lived in Chicago told me the news," DuBois said feebly. Natalie cast a wild glance at Liam—the man was obviously failing—but Liam just stared at DuBois, a glazed, fixed expression on his face, as if he was watching a car wreck and couldn't turn away from the spectacle.

"I asked her if the baby was mine," DuBois continued weakly, "but she denied it…said the baby came following her reunion with her husband. She told me we couldn't see each other after that, and we never did. It broke my heart when she told me that, just like it did when she told me that baby was her husband's. I'd hoped so much she was mine…" he said, his voice trailing off as though he were musing to himself as he sat alone in the enormous room. "Both Brigit and that little girl. I'll always remember what Brigit named her… Deidre Jean…"

It took Natalie a moment to realize that Nick Malone had entered the room and stood behind DuBois' wheelchair.

"I think you two had better go."

Liam's eyes blazed as he looked at Malone. They cooled a few degrees when he glanced back at the man in the wheelchair. DuBois' eyelids were drooping and his mouth was falling open slowly.

"Is he all right?" Liam asked, his expression masklike.

Malone nodded. "He usually falls asleep about this time in the afternoon. He tires easily. I'll call his nurse. But first…" He waved toward the door significantly.

They had no choice but to stand and leave the man in the wheelchair to his dreams.

* * *

Liam wouldn't let her drive. He was quiet when they got in the car, but calm.

"DuBois obviously has some sort of dementia," Natalie said a few minutes later as they wound their way down the private, wooded drive.

"Yeah," Liam said.

She studied his profile nervously. He'd sounded thoughtful just now, but he appeared nowhere near as shocked as she felt.

"Liam, I'm sure what he said upset you, but there's no call for accepting it as truth. You saw how confused he got at times."

"DuBois may have dementia, but his long-term memory is fine."

"You mean…you actually believe what he said about your mother and New Year's Eve and all that other stuff? But those were just some delusional beliefs coming from a man who could never have the woman he loved," Natalie exclaimed.

"I've seen it before in police investigations," Liam said levelly. "The memory for more recent events usually goes first. Sometimes DuBois remembered the name Kavanaugh, and sometimes he didn't. Long-term memory often remains quite good, though. He's never forgotten Brigit Darien."

"But—"

"This was it," he said, interrupting her.

"What was it?"

"The missing puzzle piece." Liam glanced over at her, his expression impossible for her to read. "I've got a pretty good idea now about what was happening with my father before he caused that car crash. Do you want to hear about it?"

A shiver went down her spine at his hollow tone.

"No," she whispered. The vague outline of the truth was becoming clearer and clearer now, despite the fact that she didn't want to see it…didn't want to even *consider* the fact that she'd been the one to force Liam to see it.

"Clearly it all started well before that day. Early on in their marriage, my dad must have been unfaithful to my mother. She must have found out, and fled to Tahoe in her distress… to her old friend Lincoln DuBois."

Natalie hated the flat quality to his voice, as though he spoke of strangers, not his own family.

"DuBois and my mother obviously had a brief affair, but my mother went back to Chicago and reunited with my father. Maybe since she'd been unfaithful, as well, she decided they'd both erred, and she could forgive him for what he'd done. Who knows? But they decided to commit again to their marriage, and if my observations mean anything, they were successful. They'd certainly seemed happy and devoted during my entire childhood. They moved on. Everything must have been fine until Deidre was in a boating accident and had to go into the hospital, some eighteen years after my parents' had both faltered in their marriage."

Natalie's eyes burned with unshed tears. Dread filled her chest, but her damned curiosity made her ask the question anyway.

"What has Deidre being in an accident got to do with anything?"

"The accident happened the week before my dad died. She got a cut on her leg and it severed a vein. She had to stay in the hospital for a night or two. They gave her a blood transfusion, patched her up and she was good to go. She was home before the crash ever occurred, getting up from bed against doctor's orders when my mother wasn't looking. Nobody could keep Deidre down for long," he murmured. His hands tightened on the wheel.

"Liam, pull the car over," she pleaded hoarsely, the alarm in her head starting to wail out a warning.

But he continued as if he hadn't heard her, as if he felt compelled to tell a story that had remained untold for half their lifetimes. "Somehow, my father must have become aware of something in Deidre's medical information while he was visiting her in the hospital. I don't know what, exactly, something to do with her genetics—that's why he needed to see his friend Dr. Mulonovic, the pediatric geneticist. Whatever Mulonovic told him must have confirmed his suspicions. I'm assuming my dad discovered Deidre's blood type while there in the hospital, although I can't be a hundred percent certain about that. Deidre had required a blood transfusion, so her blood type easily could have been mentioned to my dad. Blood type can't confirm paternity, but it *can* rule it out.

"I don't know if my father confronted my mother that weekend, or if he recovered our birth records and then presented them to Dr. Mulonovic. I'm thinking that's what he did. He might not have been certain about the facts, and didn't want to be wrong when he confronted my mother."

Natalie opened her eyes. Tears spilled down her cheeks.

"It must have been hell for Dad, surviving that weekend without knowing for sure, but starting to guess the truth. He and Deidre were always so close. They had such a special relationship."

His voice broke at the last.

"Liam, pull over. *Please*," Natalie said in a strangled voice.

He glanced over at her. When he saw the tears on her cheeks, he did what she asked, pulling into a gas station parking lot about a half a mile down the road. When he turned off the engine, he just sat there, his hands remaining on the steering wheel, staring out the window.

"She knew," he said quietly.

"*Who* knew?"

"My sister. Deidre. *That's* why she left Harbor Town. That's why she never came back. That's why her and Mom's relationship was severed after the crash. It wasn't because she blamed Mom for hiding Dad's drinking—or at least it wasn't just that. Deidre found out she wasn't Dad's biological daughter."

"Oh, Liam…" Natalie murmured miserably.

"Deidre was in the house with Mom when Dad came back to Harbor Town unexpectedly on that Tuesday," Liam continued in a hoarse whisper, his eyes vacant. "I was at the beach. Marc was out with Mari. Colleen was at cheerleader camp. But Deidre was there. She was supposed to stay in bed, but my mom couldn't keep her down. I'll bet she got up with her crutches when she heard Dad's voice. She must have overheard something…my dad confronting my mom…*God*… poor Deidre…how that must have hit her," he said brokenly, as if the truth had finally penetrated and he'd seen the horror of it.

Natalie put her hand on his forearm. He looked at her. A spasm of emotion went through his face. A shaky moan escaped her throat and she wrapped her arms around his shoulders, wild to comfort him…desperate in the knowledge that she'd inflicted the wound.

Chapter Fourteen

When they returned to Harbor Town, everything seemed different to Natalie. The woman who had dared less than a month ago to hire Liam Kavanaugh to investigate the crash seemed like a stranger to her now. How could she have been so bold?

How could she have been so *stupid?*

Liam dropped her off at her town house. They'd talked a great deal on their return journey, and both of them had agreed that Liam would talk to his mother about what they'd learned. There were still some pieces missing to the puzzle that only Brigit Kavanaugh could provide.

Natalie didn't envy Liam his decision to confront Brigit.

He did so on the same day they returned to Harbor Town. It was a gray September afternoon with a hint of autumn in the air. Her heart ached for Liam as she watched him drive away. He looked exhausted from their journey and the stress of what they'd learned in Tahoe.

She unpacked mechanically, telling herself not to think of the sad events of the past twenty-four hours. Every time she thought of Liam wincing in pain as they sat together in that gas station parking lot, something clenched tight in her chest. By the time she'd unpacked, coldness had settled into her bones. She went to her kitchen and filled the tea kettle. As she stared blankly out the window over her sink, it all seemed to crash into her like an emotional tidal wave.

She lowered her head and sobbed.

It hurt like hell, knowing full well what she'd done. Others had been able to quiet their curiosity about the crash. Mari had never seen fit to hire an investigator. Eric had never obsessed the way Natalie did.

Why couldn't she have just let it rest? Now it was done, and she had to live with the knowledge that her obsession had wounded the man she care for—loved—more than anything in the world.

She hadn't just hurt Liam with her actions, either. She'd started events that would lead to all the Kavanaugh children questioning their parents, their pasts, the very foundations of their lives. They would think her malicious in her interference.

She'd gained what she thought she'd wanted, and in doing so, she'd sacrificed the real treasure. Liam.

After she'd cried herself dry, she felt hollowed out…empty. The knowledge of what she had to do left her numb.

A knock sounded after ten o'clock that evening. Outwardly, she was composed as she answered the door. Inwardly, it was as if an icy hand clutched her heart.

"How did it go?" Natalie asked a minute later, once Liam had settled tiredly in an easy chair in her living room, and she'd brought him a cup of coffee, at his request.

He exhaled heavily and took a large sip of the hot drink. "Well…my mom didn't deny any of it. We've been talking nonstop the entire time. Once she understood that I knew the truth about DuBois, she sort of just...broke."

"Is she all right?" Natalie asked, concerned.

Liam nodded. "Yeah. I'm not saying it was easy on her, but I think she's okay. I called Colleen, and she and the kids came to stay with her tonight. I had no idea..."

"What?" Natalie whispered.

"I had no idea how guilty she always felt. Mom feels it was all her fault—the crash, the deaths, Deidre's fury at her." He gave her an entreating look. "It was always there, eating away at her. That's why she was so defensive, why she was so...hard. I didn't mention this to her, but I think it could be why she wasn't taking her medications last year, why she was letting her health go. I think part of her didn't care anymore...."

"It's so strange," Natalie said quietly as she sat down on the couch. "To think mistakes we made years ago could come back and affect us so greatly."

Liam rubbed his whiskered jaw tiredly. "To think they could affect family, but also complete strangers. It's a hell of a thing."

Natalie nodded. "So what now?"

"I have to go to Germany. I have to talk to Deidre. According to my mother, Deidre *did* overhear the confrontation between my father and mother. I was right about that. The awful thing about it is, she overheard my father accusing my mom of Deidre being another man's child, and my mother admitting it could be true. My father told Mom about the blood types—he assured her it *was* true. Deidre *couldn't* be his. But Deidre never heard the identity of her biological father. My mom said she got upset and hurried away when she heard that she—you know—wasn't my dad's. Deidre demanded to know who her biological father was later, but my mother refused to tell her. She begged Deidre just to accept that Derry was the only person who had ever been her father."

Liam paused and dug his fingertips into his closed eyelids. He looked so exhausted—both physically and emotionally. Natalie longed to touch him, but she remained motionless. She felt as if she'd lost the right to comfort him.

"Deidre told Mom she was right. 'Derry will always be my father—it's *you* who aren't my mother anymore.' I told you how close my dad and Deidre were. Deidre must have felt like Mom robbed her of that. I suppose the feeling amplified a hundredfold after the crash."

Natalie couldn't think of how to respond to so much hurt and misery.

"My mom admitted that she told Dad on the day of the crash that she'd had a brief affair with Lincoln DuBois. That's why my dad must have been so destroyed when he saw DuBois on the news. He was already upset, but seeing DuBois' face must have twisted the knife. Apparently, Mom told Dad she hadn't suspected Deidre was Linc's child over the years, but she told me tonight she had her suspicions all along. Deidre not only had a different blood type from Marc, Colleen and I, she also had a very rare type. Mom had gotten hints from the medical staff when she gave birth that the blood typing for the baby didn't match Mom's and Dad's blood types. Mom managed to keep that quiet over the years, until Deidre's accident."

He opened his eyes and their stares met.

"I have to go to tell Deidre who her biological father is. She would want to know."

"*Lincoln* would want to know."

Liam nodded grimly. "You saw how sick he was. There may not be enough time. I'll have to leave tonight. Besides... I'm due to start work next week. If I'm going to go, I have to do it now."

Natalie nodded. "I'll get you some more coffee."

"I don't want anymore coffee. I want to hold you. Come here."

She swallowed thickly and remained on the couch. His brow furrowed.

"What's wrong?" he asked.

"Liam...I can't tell you how sorry I am. About everything," she whispered.

"None of this is your fault."

She laughed raggedly. His expression froze at the desperate sound.

"It's *all* my fault, and you know it," she whispered, staring blankly at the painting about her fireplace. From the corner of her eye, she saw him rise. She stood abruptly, sensing he was coming over to the couch to comfort her. His touch would shatter her. She turned her shoulder to him and walked several steps away.

"Natalie...what's going on?" he asked slowly.

"This thing between us...it's not going to work out, Liam," she said, averting her gaze. She cringed inwardly in the ensuing silence.

"I don't follow you. Why?"

"Do you really have to ask that? Your family has been changed forever because of me. Your mother must be furious. Deidre is going to be flattened." She glanced back at him furtively. His face looked rigid with tension. "It's not just that," she whispered.

"What, then?" he demanded.

Her bark of laughter bordered on a sob. She waved her hand between them. "You and I together. It's...it's ridiculous. Surely you see that. We're not...suited."

"I couldn't disagree more," he replied stiffly. "You didn't think so just a few days ago, either."

"You're wrong," she said more emphatically. She ignored

the tear spilling down her cheek. It was imperative that she make him understand this. She couldn't bear to consider him furthering this huge mistake they'd made…the error *she'd* made. He was about to have so many new, unpleasant truths start to crash in on him. She couldn't stand to think of him enduring that while he was still involved with her—the instigator of his unhappiness. "I've been thinking it for a while now. I spoke to my brother about it just before we left for Reno."

She looked away from his narrowed gaze, fearful he would see the lie in her eyes. She had spoken to Eric, and Eric had given his opinion on his doubts about her affair with Liam. Natalie had refused to listen to a word of it.

"Eric and I agreed that what was happening between you and me was an emotional backlash, given everything that's happened in the past," she said, forcing her voice not to tremble.

"You and Eric agreed on that, huh?"

"Yes."

"Look in my eyes and tell me that, Natalie," he said, a hard edge to his quiet voice.

She inhaled, willing the pain in her chest and throat to ease. She looked into his eyes.

"It was a mistake, Liam. All of it."

For a few seconds, he just studied her. A pressure in her grew, a wild need to fly into his arms and take it all back. It swelled in her chest when he turned and headed toward the front door.

She stood motionless for a full two minutes after he'd left, waiting for the pain to diminish. It eventually grew into a dull ache that felt like a cold, hard stone pressing against her heart.

Several days passed, and Natalie did the things she always did—she went to work, she went to a dance class, she had dinner with her brother, Eric, one night. She felt like a robot, though. Empty. Lonely.

Once, she'd given in to a shameful melancholy and gone to Liam's empty cottage. She'd sat on the terrace, where they'd spent so many happy hours together, and she'd cried like the foolish child she'd been just one month before.

She'd once told Liam that he was worried she'd asked him to open Pandora's box. That's precisely what had happened. Surely on his solitary journey to Germany, Liam would realize that. He would see the truth of what she'd said when she'd broken up with him. The circumstances of their investigation had not only thrown them together repeatedly, but had created a unique, emotionally charged atmosphere; one in which he might mistake his sympathy for the victim of his father's crime for feelings of desire and caring.

Now that Natalie was alone and had time to reflect, she could find no other good explanation for what had occurred between her and Liam.

Not on his part, anyway. For her part, it was simple. She'd fallen hopelessly, completely in love.

Eric had been right about another thing. Liam Kavanaugh could get practically any woman he wanted on the planet. He was bound to eventually break her heart. Perhaps it was best for that wound to come sooner versus later, so that she could begin healing.

Both Liam and she needed to start the process of healing.

On the fourth night after Liam had left Harbor Town, Natalie woke in a sweat. Summerlike weather had returned with a vengeance. The last few days had been hot and muggy. She considered getting up and turning on the air-conditioning, but instead rose and opened her bureau for clothes.

She threw on some shorts and a tank top and hurriedly brushed her hair, leaving it down. The moon shone especially bright on Travertine Road as she drove. She parked her car in the empty public parking lot.

She finally caught the cool lake breeze she sought as she walked onto White Sands, barefoot. For a full half hour, she sat on the desolate beach and listened to the waves rolling in, regular and steady as her breath. After a while, she couldn't bear the stillness a moment longer.

She stood, and let her anguish move her.

It wasn't uncommon for her to dance on White Sands when she was troubled. Tonight her emotions compelled her to new heights. She spun with longing; she leaped higher because she craved so much; her feet were compelled by the knowledge of love and desire, and by the fear that she might never know it again.

And when she stopped moving, she saw the object of her desire standing on the beach, watching her. She froze in her posture, sure for a moment he was an illusion conjured from her longing and moonlight. He stepped toward her and suddenly he was a solid man…even more wondrous than the fantasy of him.

She took one hesitant step toward him.

"What are you doing here?" she asked Liam.

"I went to your place the second I got back from the airport. Then I looked around town for you, and finally saw your car here, in the parking lot."

His low voice sounded wonderful to her ears, if a little surreal. She'd longed to hear it so many times in the past few days.

"I thought a lot about what you said…about it being a mistake for us to have gotten together. I had plenty of time to think while I was on that plane for all those hours."

"Oh?" Natalie asked shakily. She saw him nod.

"At first, I was just mad as hell. Somewhere over the Atlantic Ocean, I started to think a little more rationally. By the time I stewed over things on the return trip, I came to a few conclusions. You had your say the other day. How about if you give me a chance to say my piece now?"

"I suppose that's only fair," Natalie murmured as her heart started to pound loudly in her ears.

"Do you remember early on, when you told me I shouldn't assume I was going to learn something that would make me love my father less? That I might learn something to make me love him more?"

Natalie lowered her head in shame.

"You shouldn't feel bad about saying that, Natalie. Because it was the truth."

Her head came up.

"Before you, I couldn't fully *see* my mother and father. I couldn't see them like an adult sees another adult. I was blinded by secrets and hurt. Because of you, I'm seeing them as three-dimensional people who made mistakes, and suffered, and who still managed to love and be loved. I'm seeing their flaws—trust me, I see them clearly—but I'm seeing their humanity more than ever, as well. You gave me that, Natalie."

She stifled a sob.

"And I started to realize something else on that plane. I know how uncertain you've been at times about us being together. I know you haven't had that much experience with guys. I started to think maybe after what happened in Lake Tahoe, your guilt and your insecurity got the better of you. I started to think—well, *hope,* I guess—maybe you'd made a decision about breaking up based on those things," he said, his voice growing gruff. "And not about what was really in your heart."

The sob finally escaped her throat. She took one step, and suddenly he'd closed the distance between them in the blink of an eye.

"Natalie."

That was all Liam said. One word, whispered hoarsely against her neck, and tears of joy burst from her eyes, because all the distilled longing in his voice was more powerful than all the doubts she'd had ever since he'd gone...

All the doubts she'd collected in a lifetime.

"I missed you so much," she said.

He rubbed her back, as if signaling for her to look at him. She lifted her head and saw that a small smile shaped his firm mouth.

"I think I must have first fallen in love with you when I saw you dancing on this beach," he murmured.

Her laugh sounded ragged with mingled disbelief and joy.

"Do you know what I think we should do?" Liam asked her quietly.

She shook her head. It was impossible for her to speak at the moment, as full as her heart felt.

"I think we should turn George Myerson's saloon into a dance studio. That way I won't always be driving down to White Sands when I wake up in the middle of the night and find you gone from bed. And you know what else?"

"What?" she asked wetly.

"I don't think you should spend another night anywhere but in my arms. *Ever.*"

Fresh tears spilled down her face.

His expression softened when he fully took in how overwhelmed she was.

"Why are you crying?" he whispered.

"I thought...I thought maybe you wouldn't be able to forgive me. I thought it was just a matter of time before you saw it was all a big mistake."

"So you decided to be the one to end things?"

Natalie nodded, feeling foolish. "It hurt so much to let you go," she said shakily. "I was stupid. I hope you understand. I was the one who caused you all this grief. Before me, you'd considered your parents' marriage solid...sanctified. Before me, Deidre was your full sister, not your half one."

"Deidre will always be my sister. Completely," he said quietly, brushing tears off her cheeks with his thumb. "Nothing can change that. I only wish my father could have given himself time to reflect. He would always be Deidre's father. Always."

He placed his hand at the back of her head and brought her head down so he could land several hungry kisses on her mouth. "You were *right* to do what you did. You and I had nothing to do with the events that led up to that crash, but we had a right to know why it happened. I'm *glad* you asked me to look into this."

"You are?" she breathed out in wonder.

"Oh, yeah," he said certainly before he gently placed her feet on the ground, keeping their bodies pressed close. "You were the one who prodded me into doing what I should have done a long time ago. I'm thankful for that, more thankful than you'll ever know. It hasn't been easy, but stuff like this rarely is, I guess."

She stared up at his face cast in moonlight, thinking he was the most miraculous thing she'd ever seen in her life.

"Is Deidre okay? Did you tell her about Linc?"

"Yeah. She's flying to Tahoe even as we speak. I saw her off in Detroit."

"You're kidding."

Liam shook his head.

"But surely she shouldn't go alone," Natalie murmured.

He sighed. "No one needs to take care of Deidre. She's a force of nature. I told her I'd come out and join her in a few days if she wanted me there. Who knows what's going to happen? We'll just have to let things play out as far as her and Linc. I wanted to get back to Harbor Town as soon as possible, though."

"Why? Because of your job?"

"No. Because I couldn't stand not seeing you another second longer," he said with a low, sexy chuckle that caused goose bumps to rise on her neck. He shook his head in bemusement as he looked down at her. "I wonder if I'll ever figure you out." He cupped her jaw in his customary tender gesture. A few more tears spilled down her cheek onto his fingers. "Did you really have yourself convinced this was a temporary thing between us? A blip on the radar screen?"

She winced. "I didn't want to believe it, but the circumstances have been so strange. I thought maybe..."

"What?" he demanded gently.

"That you'd convinced yourself you cared, when really it was just misplaced guilt...or pity," she finished in a whisper.

She caught the fierce glint in his eyes before he lowered his head and spoke next to her upturned lips.

"The last thing I feel toward you is pity. Will you get that into your head?"

He raised his eyebrows in half exasperation, half amusement when she nodded meekly. He pressed his forehead next to hers.

"There are a lot of things that are uncertain for my family right now. Please tell me you're a certainty, Natalie."

"I'm a certainty," she replied quickly.

His slow grin caused a quivery sensation deep inside her.

"*Good.* Because I've never been more certain of anything in my life. How about if we go to the cottage...how about if we go home?"

She couldn't help but grin. "Eric is going to be so put off by all this."

"To hell with Eric," Liam said. "He shouldn't have ever

tried to talk you out of living at the cottage, when it's obvious it's your home."

They shared a smile.

"You ready?"

"I'm so ready," she whispered.

His mouth lowered, and they sealed their deal with a kiss.

* * * * *

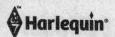

COMING NEXT MONTH

Available August 30, 2011

SPECIAL EDITION®

REQUEST YOUR FREE BOOKS!
2 FREE NOVELS PLUS 2 FREE GIFTS!

◆ Harlequin

SPECIAL EDITION
Life, Love & Family

YES! Please send me 2 FREE Harlequin® Special Edition novels and my 2 FREE gifts (gifts are worth about $10). After receiving them, if I don't wish to receive any more books, I can return the shipping statement marked "cancel." If I don't cancel, I will receive 6 brand-new novels every month and be billed just $4.49 per book in the U.S. or $5.24 per book in Canada. That's a saving of at least 14% off the cover price! It's quite a bargain! Shipping and handling is just 50¢ per book in the U.S. and 75¢ per book in Canada.* I understand that accepting the 2 free books and gifts places me under no obligation to buy anything. I can always return a shipment and cancel at any time. Even if I never buy another book, the two free books and gifts are mine to keep forever.

235/335 HDN FEGF

Name	(PLEASE PRINT)

Address		Apt. #

City	State/Prov.	Zip/Postal Code

Signature (if under 18, a parent or guardian must sign)

Mail to the **Reader Service**:
IN U.S.A.: P.O. Box 1867, Buffalo, NY 14240-1867
IN CANADA: P.O. Box 609, Fort Erie, Ontario L2A 5X3

Not valid for current subscribers to Harlequin Special Edition books.

Want to try two free books from another line?
Call 1-800-873-8635 or visit www.ReaderService.com.

* Terms and prices subject to change without notice. Prices do not include applicable taxes. Sales tax applicable in N.Y. Canadian residents will be charged applicable taxes. Offer not valid in Quebec. This offer is limited to one order per household. All orders subject to credit approval. Credit or debit balances in a customer's account(s) may be offset by any other outstanding balance owed by or to the customer. Please allow 4 to 6 weeks for delivery. Offer available while quantities last.

HSE11B

New York Times *and* USA TODAY *bestselling author*
Maya Banks presents a brand-new miniseries

PREGNANCY & PASSION

When four irresistible tycoons face
the consequences of temptation.

Book 1—ENTICED BY HIS FORGOTTEN LOVER

Available September 2011 from Harlequin® Desire®!

Rafael de Luca had been in bad situations before. A crowded ballroom could never make him sweat.

These people would never know that he had no memory of any of them.

He surveyed the party with grim tolerance, searching for the source of his unease.

At first his gaze flickered past her, but he yanked his attention back to a woman across the room. Her stare bored holes through him. Unflinching and steady, even when his eyes locked with hers.

Petite, even in heels, she had a creamy olive complexion. A wealth of inky-black curls cascaded over her shoulders and her eyes were equally dark.

She looked at him as if she'd already judged him and found him lacking. He'd never seen her before in his life. Or had he?

He cursed the gaping hole in his memory. He'd been diagnosed with selective amnesia after his accident four months ago. Which seemed like complete and utter bull. No one got amnesia except hysterical women in bad soap operas.

With a smile, he disengaged himself from the group

around him and made his way to the mystery woman.

She wasn't coy. She stared straight at him as he approached, her chin thrust upward in defiance.

"Excuse me, but have we met?" he asked in his smoothest voice.

His gaze moved over the generous swell of her breasts pushed up by the empire waist of her black cocktail dress.

When he glanced back up at her face, he saw fury in her eyes.

"Have we *met?*" Her voice was barely a whisper, but he felt each word like the crack of a whip.

Before he could process her response, she nailed him with a right hook. He stumbled back, holding his nose.

One of his guards stepped between Rafe and the woman, accidentally sending her to one knee. Her hand flew to the folds of her dress.

It was then, as she cupped her belly, that the realization hit him. She was pregnant.

Her eyes flashing, she turned and ran down the marble hallway.

Rafael ran after her. He burst from the hotel lobby, and saw two shoes sparkling in the moonlight, twinkling at him.

He blew out his breath in frustration and then shoved the pair of sparkly, ultrafeminine heels at his head of security.

"Find the woman who wore these shoes."

Will Rafael find his mystery woman?
Find out in Maya Banks's passionate new novel
ENTICED BY HIS FORGOTTEN LOVER
Available September 2011 from Harlequin® Desire®!

HDEXP0911

Love and family secrets collide in
a powerful new trilogy from

Linda Warren

the Hardin Boys

Blood is thicker than oil

Coming August 9, 2011.

The Texan's Secret

Before Chance Hardin can join his brothers in
their new oil business, he must reveal a secret
that could tear their family apart. And his
desire for family has never been stronger, all
because of beautiful Shay Dumont.
A woman with a secret of her own....

The Texan's Bride
(October 11, 2011)

The Texan's Christmas
(December 6, 2011)

Harlequin® *Romance*

Discover small-town warmth and community spirit
in a brand-new trilogy from

PATRICIA THAYER

The Quilt Shop in **KERRY SPRINGS**

*Where dreams
are stitched…patch
by patch!*

Coming August 9, 2011.

Little Cowgirl Needs a Mom

Warm-spirited quilt shop owner Jenny Collins promises to
help little Gracie finish the quilt her late mother started,
even if it means butting heads with Gracie's father,
grumpy but gorgeous rancher Evan Rafferty….

The Lonesome Rancher
(September 13, 2011)

Tall, Dark, Texas Ranger
(October 11, 2011)

Harlequin®

ROMANTIC
SUSPENSE

NEW YORK TIMES BESTSELLING AUTHOR
RACHEL LEE

The Rescue Pilot

Time is running out…

Desperate to help her ailing sister, Rory is determined
to get Cait the necessary treatment to help her fight
a devastating disease. A cross-country trip turns into
a fight for survival in more ways than one when their plane
encounters trouble. Can Rory trust pilot Chase Dakota
with their lives, and possibly her heart?

**Look for this heart-stopping romance in September
from *New York Times* bestselling author Rachel Lee
and Harlequin Romantic Suspense!**

Conard
County *THE NEXT
GENERATION*

Available in September wherever books are sold!

www.Harlequin.com.

RSRL27741